A Testament in Purgatory

M. Kevin Durak
&
Scott D. Muck

PUBLISH AMERICA

PublishAmerica
Baltimore

First printing

At the specific preference of the author, PublishAmerica allowed this work to remain exactly as the author intended, verbatim, without editorial input.

ISBN: 1-4241-1895-6
PUBLISHED BY PUBLISHAMERICA, LLLP
www.publishamerica.com
Baltimore

Printed in the United States of America

Chapter 1
Magnus

"Coffee, black and hot."

"Good morning, Magnus."

I looked into the eyes of the girl behind the counter. She had brown eyes. Brown eyes were the hardest to read, and fittingly, I could not get a read on her. I wondered how she knew my name. She did not look familiar. It probably had something to do with the fact that I had been going to that coffeehouse five times a week for over two years. I was usually the first customer in the store when it opened in the morning. I had probably become a familiar face to her. But to me, she did not look familiar.

"One large coffee," she said as she put the cup of coffee on the counter. "It will be one ninety-five."

"Okay," I replied as I threw the money on the counter. She probably thought it to be rude. Truth being told...it probably was.

"You're a bad boy aren't you, Magnus?" she said as she scooped the change from the counter.

"Excuse me?" I replied as I grabbed the hot cup of coffee, making sure her hand was out of the way.

"You are one of those guys my mother warned me about, aren't you?"

"More like the one your priest warned you about."

"Enjoy your coffee," she mumbled with a confused look upon her face.

3

I quickly turned to get away from the situation. I always had trouble saying "thank you", or "good-bye", or pretty much anything that would be considered "courteous". It was something I did not like to do. Nor could I stand touching anyone. Handshakes, kisses, and any other physical pleasantries always bothered me. The situation with this girl had become increasingly uncomfortable, and I needed to get away from it.

As I turned away, I caught a glimpse of someone who was familiar: the coffeehouse manager. I am not sure why he looked familiar to me. He was tall, but not exceptionally tall. He was around thirty years old. He was clean cut, with short black hair. The one thing unique about him was that his skin was somewhat pale. He had been running the coffeehouse for a few months. His presence always made me uneasy. Whenever he served me, he would give me my coffee and go back to work. He never gave me a chance to look him in the eyes, but I always felt like he was watching me. He had dark, brown eyes, which were always the hardest to read. He was someone I did not like. I felt that I knew him from long ago, or from a time I could not remember. I knew that was unlikely, but I had a strange feeling about him. Maybe it was something else, like how he changed the café when he became manager. He brought in all new decorations, new specials, and new employees. It was a complete change to the environment in the coffeehouse that I had become accustomed to. At least the coffee was the same. I think that was the reason I continued to go into the coffeehouse. I liked the coffee. It was my routine, and I was used to it. I realized I was lingering. I had to get to work. I quickly walked to the door of the coffeehouse and exited.

As I walked the sidewalk that led to the store I worked at, I ripped off the lid on the coffee. It was hot, scolding hot, the way I liked it. It was kind of ironic I bought coffee everyday from the coffeehouse. Sure I worked next door, but I worked for a food supplier and we supplied the coffee to them. I could have just made coffee at work everyday and saved myself the dollar ninety-five. But for some reason the coffeehouse made it the way I liked it. It bothered me, though. I was always one who believed in efficiency, practicality, and common sense. Yet, everyday I bought coffee from them. At least it was not an espresso, or even worse, a latte.

I walked through the automatic doors at the entrance to the marketplace. Three women that worked at the marketplace turned to look at me. Not a single one was wearing their uniform correctly. It did not surprise me. Not a single person did. One was missing her name badge, another had loop earrings and was chewing gum, and the last was not wearing an apron. All of them had their shirts untucked.

"Good morning, Magnus."

It was tradition for the cashiers to say "good morning" to me as I walked in the door. The truth was I did not like them, and they must not have liked me. They were just being polite. I did not like being polite. Every morning they would say "good morning", and every morning I would walk right by them. That morning was no exception. I went to work stocking the store.

It was a grocery store that sold items in large quantities. It was a small store having only seven aisles, a freezer, and a cooler. Most of the time the cashiers stayed up at the front of the store near the registers or the front desk. They sat around and complained about the customers, the stockers, the store manager, and everything else they could think of while they ate cookies and donuts and wondered why their asses kept getting bigger. These were the reasons why I tried to avoid the front of the store at all times. I usually worked the rest of the store. The job was easy and required little interaction with others. I was the Operations Manager, and had held the position for over two years. Two years that most would call boring. But I did not mind. I did not mind getting coffee every morning. I did not mind working the same job everyday. I did not mind going home to an empty apartment every night. I liked that no one asked me questions. It was just what I was looking for.

One thing was different that day. I had made small talk with the girl at the coffee store. That one thing kept running through my mind. *Why did she call me by my name? Was she just being polite?* I had noticed that people could be polite quite often. Still, no one had made small talk with me during the past two years that I had been going into the coffeehouse.

She was attractive, but I was quite sure I was not attracted to her. I think I was attracted to the idea of her interest in me. It was something quite different for me. I spent most of the morning contemplating what had happened at the coffee shop as I slowly stocked the product in the grocery aisles.

Why would the girl say hello to me? Did she find me attractive? I do not think I was ever considered good looking. My short, blonde hair was like many others. I was of average height. I was of average weight. Nothing was very special about my appearance...accept my eyes. *Could it be my eyes?* They were dark blue. I had heard people in the past say "so-and-so" has pretty blue eyes. But never mine. No one ever gave me a complement, and surely never one about my appearance.

"Excuse me, sir," a woman customer said, interrupting my train of thought.

"Yes?" I asked as I turned to face her. She was middle-aged with dyed brown hair that was so thin that it looked like it was about to fall out. She wore too much make-up, and was dressed in a bright red jump suit. Her eyes told a different story than her appearance. She had strength and pride in her eyes. She probably had a very acceptable youth filled with joyous occasions. She was probably a very good-looking woman then, and was trying to hold on to something that no longer existed. I never understood why people did that.

"Where do I go to get this sliced?" she asked, pointing into her cart.

I looked into her cart and saw that she had a deli-style turkey. One of the services the marketplace offered was free meat slicing. All the employees thought it was a hassle, and they all made an effort to make sure the customer knew it was a hassle. Only the Store Manager was ever polite to the customers about it. I think it was because he never did the slicing. He always made me, or one of the stockers do it.

"I can take it for you," I told her. "How would you like it sliced?" I knew the answer before she said it. Every customer answered that question the same. "Thin, but not too thin."

No one knew what that meant. No matter how it was sliced, it never fit that description. "For sandwiches?" I asked, trying to help clarify how she wanted the turkey cut.

"Yes."

"I will have it done in a few minutes," I told her as I took the turkey.

I slowly made my way to the slicer. I did not want to slice the turkey. I wanted to go back to stocking the store and thinking about the girl at the coffeehouse. *Why did she say hello to me?*

I saw the morning stocker standing by the front counter doing nothing. I knew he would be an excellent candidate to slice this turkey.

"Donald," I called to him. He was one of the older stockers, but his attitude was even worse toward the store then the younger ones. He saw the turkey and frowned. He knew what was coming next.

"Yeah?" he replied, rudely.

"Can you slice this for the customer in aisle one?"

"God dammit. I just did one."

"Well, make sure you clean the slicer," I said as I handed him the turkey.

"Fine."

I never understood why people had to swear for the most minute of reasons. All he had to do was slice a turkey. Yet, he had to break the second commandment to show his disapproval.

I turned around and headed back to aisle one. I passed the customer on the way.

"Your turkey will be done in a few minutes."

"Thank you."

I went back to stocking the store. It was afternoon by the time I was first bothered by the cashiers that day.

"Magnus to the front!" blared over the store intercom.

I slowly made my way to the front of the store. The slower I walked, the angrier the cashier would be by the time I got to the front of the store. One of the few things I enjoyed was irritating the cashiers.

"Can I help you?" I asked one of the older cashiers, I believe her name was Jan. It was hard to remember since she hardly wore her name badge.

"Yes, this man needs three cases of party wings," she said as she pointed over my shoulder.

I turned to see a fat man with a dirty apron. I did not want to know what the filth was that had stained the white apron he wore. I was quite sure that some of it was his sweat.

"Hey, Magnus, you get me my stuff?" the fat man said with a heavy accent.

"Yes, I will be back in a moment."

I walked to the back of the store and into the back room. The door to the freezer was through the back room. I opened the door of the freezer and walked inside. I always hated going into the freezer. I hated the cold. I quickly grabbed the three cases of party wings and walked out of the freezer and into the backroom.

I looked up to see the fat man waiting for me. He obviously could not hear because I told him I would be back in a moment. He obviously could not read since the door to back room blatantly said "EMPLOYEES ONLY".

"Yo, cuz," the fat man said as he stuck out his arms. I dumped the cases in his arms and he struggled to carry them. If he were a smart man, he would have gotten a shopping cart on his way to the back. It was a typical customer: stupid, could not read, and in a hurry.

"Is that all?" I asked.

"Yeah," he blurted as he tried to balance the cases while walking out of the back room. I hoped he would not fall over. I did not want to clean the blood and grease off the floor.

I went back to stocking the store. I needed to make sure the store looked well stocked by the time the Store Manager came in. If the store looked good when he arrived, then he would not have to talk to me. The less he talked to me, the better. The less I talk to anyone, the better. Except for the girl at the coffeehouse. I could not get her out of my head. *Did I want to get her out of my head?* I wanted to go back to the coffeehouse and talk to her some more. I could not figure out why.

On my way back to the aisle I was working in, an older lady grabbed my arm and asked, "What's the difference between the meatballs?"

Instinct pulled my arm away from her. "Excuse me?" I said rudely.

"What's the difference between the meatballs?" she asked again, growing impatient.

"The ones on the top shelf are the premium. They have more meat, and thus are more expensive. The ones on the lower shelf are the regular style. They have more filler and thus are less expensive. People say they taste the same after they are simmered in sauce."

"Okay," she retorted as she reached for the cheap ones on the bottom shelf.

9

Customers had become very predictable to me. They were impatient and believed they were never wrong. Working at the marketplace gave me an insight into the human race that no college class could ever teach. As I interacted with the customers, I became increasingly aware of their lack of manners. Not many said "please" or "thank you", some stole from the store, the rest were pushy to each other and to the employees. They demanded the most trivial things, and complained constantly.

I walked back to the aisle I was working in without further incident. It would only be for a few moments. About ten minutes later I was interrupted again.

"Hey, Magnus."

I turned to see one of our stock boys walking up the aisle toward me. He apparently forgot to shave today, and he was wearing an earring. Both were infractions of our dress code. Like all of our employees, he seemed to lack the necessary skills to tuck in his shirt.

"How much did you get done?" he asked as he walked up to me.

I looked at him for a moment not saying a word. Of all the faults that the customers possessed, the employees were worse. They were always rude to the customers and to the managers. They did not like their jobs, and they had no qualms in concealing their dislike. Most were young high school or college students who only worked because their parents made them. The stockers were rude and lazy, but they did do work from time to time. The one thing I liked about them was that they seldom complained. I guess they did not have much to complain about as they walked around the store ignoring customers and drinking pop. The stockers were bad, but the cashiers were probably the worst collection of human beings I had ever met. They never did any work except push some buttons and scan the customers' items. They were always rude, and always complained.

"I did aisles one and two," I replied to the stock boy.

"Sweet, not much left to do then."

"You will most likely have to go through them again at the end of the day..."

He did not hear me. He had already turned around and was walking toward the front of the store. It was shift change and the older cashiers were leaving and the young high school and college girls were coming in. It was a daily ritual for the stockers to flirt with the cashiers as they walked in and got ready for work. It seemed both sides enjoyed it. I think it may have been the only thing they liked about working. I never made a fuss about it. The other managers always broke it up and told everyone to get to work. Luckily, the employees were no concern to me. As Operations Manager, my job was to make the store look good and make sure the product sold. The Store Manager and his Assistant could worry all they wanted about employee productivity and customer relations, I had more than my fair share of that in the past.

I saw the Store Manager standing at the end of the aisle telling the employees to get to work. It was time for me to go. I walked up to him and fixed my tie while he finished talking.

"...And make sure you guys take the trash from the garbage can out front," the Store Manager yelled to the stockers as he turned to face me. "Hello, Magnus. Busy this morning?"

"Somewhat slow, but I did not get much done. I only got to aisles one and two. They were really bad. I don't think anyone did them last night."

"That's okay, Magnus."

He knew as well as I did that he never checked to see if the stockers worked the aisles. It happened a lot. Everything that was wrong with the store was a direct cause of management. The Store Manager did not care about anything, nor would he ever. The employees seemed to follow that lead. The only one who ever did their job right was me.

I nodded to the Store Manager and walked out the front door. My apartment was not far and I always walked to and from work. I walked slower than usual that day on my way to my apartment. I needed to figure out what to say to the girl at the coffeehouse the next time I talked to her.

Chapter 2
Samuel

As you sit and stare into space, during one of many times at work that you are bored, or have nothing better to do, do you often second guess if this is actually the job you are meant to do? Well, that's what used to go through my head. My name is Samuel. For the past six months, I have stared into space on countless occasions. I spent years searching the earth for that one thing. I could not find it. I tried job after job, searching for anything that might bring me fulfillment. I tried college, the army, and various odd jobs throughout the years. If nothing else, it gave me a great sense of the variety that this world can offer.

My most recent position was as a manager of a coffeehouse. This meaningless—yet somewhat fulfilling—job, gave me the opportunity to watch caffeine-addicted people pollute themselves day in and day out with brown, acidic liquids. I had to make sure the kids made the coffee right every day. The right amount of beans with the proper grind and the customers will come back for more. That is what it is all about here—get them addicted and they will keep spending. Maybe it is some universal law. I prefer tea.

The owners of the coffeehouse hired me to bring their dying business to life. They opened the place over two years ago and kept sinking money into it with no results. They had tried a number of themes, gimmicks, and managers, but nothing seemed to work. It seemed, by hiring me they were simply looking to finally bring order to the chaos they created. I was enthusiastic about this idea. When I started, I reinvented most of the café. The place already had a safari look to it, but I came up with new drinks, uniforms, and events. I even fired all but one of the staff and hired new employees.

I would arrive everyday and do a quick check of the place, making sure that the night crew swept and mopped properly. Three booths on the left side; four along the right wall; and six tables, with two to four chairs each adorned the slate tile walkway through the center of the café. The counter was in the back left portion of the store. The kids did a good job cleaning every night, but I checked anyhow. I had to make it seem like my job was more important than it really was.

When you work as a manager, you come to realize that you hire people who have a little bit of you in them. Or you just hire someone based on looks. Ultimately, you want to work with people that you like. That is one of the luxuries of being the person in charge of hiring. You get to choose who you work with. Of course, they have to choose to work for you.

The walls afforded me the opportunity to get lost in a world far away. It was like a little piece of the jungle had been cut out of a rain forest and put on display for the masses. Giant printed banana leaves set against an eerie black and gray backdrop. If I stared at it long enough, which I had plenty of time to do, the leaves would start to look like green fire engulfing the entire café. Then, after hours of staring at green fire, my eyes would be diverted to the animal-like features of the booths and decorations. Leopard skin print booths, a mirror danced upon by tiny elephants, and animal print end tables were jumbled together in no discernable pattern throughout the store.

The coffeehouse was located in a plaza with a few other stores and a large asphalt parking lot. The intersection the plaza was located on was one of the busier crossroads in town. At nine and five the streets were jammed—people going to and from work. Everyone's doing something important…or so I thought. I would often try to rationalize what was so important to these people. In turn I looked upon the significance of my being here and this situation…serving coffee.

"Maybe today will be the day," I whispered to myself, as a girl walked into the coffeehouse. She glided across the slate tile floor. She shined up the dullness of the slate. Nameless, just like the rest, but she embodied something unique. Bright eyes…her stare…her smile…

She introduced herself. "Hi, I'm Sarah. Is Amy here?" I forgot her name instantly. They are all nameless to me when I first meet them.

Amy, one of the new girls at work, came out from the back room. "Hey, Sarah," she said exuberantly, then turned to me. "This is my friend. She will probably be coming in a lot. She has nothing better to do, so she told me she would be visiting. And this is my brother," she added, pointing to the guy next to the nameless wonder.

"Hello," I said, shaking Amy's brother's hand. I was scared to touch the nameless girl.

"This is my manager, Samuel," Amy said.

"How are you doing today?" I asked. Words never seemed right when I wanted them to have meaning.

"We're good," Amy's brother chimed in.

I guessed from his response that he was dating Amy's friend. I didn't want to be polite, anymore. "Can I get you anything today?" I mumbled.

"We'll have two coffees," the nameless beauty replied.

Her voice gave my ears a tickle. This was a new sensation for me.

However, my instinct for duty prevailed. "That'll be three ninety," I said. Amy's brother handed the money to me. "Enjoy your coffees," I added, handing back their change. It was just like every other transaction. I become a drone after doing a mindless job long enough.

"Thank you."

Watching her move away from the counter was almost as alluring as watching her come to it. She was dressed in a tight white tank top and somewhat loose fitting jeans. She had sandals on, revealing beautiful feet. Her hair was clean with a look of nonchalance. It looked like she had just got out of the shower. A new and strange feeling engulfed my body.

"Can I take a break? I want to sit down with my friend and brother," Amy inquired.

"No problem," I replied. "I'll be right back. Just keep an eye out for customers."

She nodded.

I stepped through the saloon doors and into the back room. I made my way to the bathroom. I bent my knees slightly so I could look into the mirror. The mirror reflected the inevitable fact that I was nobody here. I loosened my tie. I looked at my hair, which matched the darkness of my eyes. I could never decide on a hairstyle. I usually just kept it short so I didn't have to think about. "Maybe if my hair is combed right she will like me," I said to myself in the mirror.

I looked closely at my large nose. A pimple must have formed sometime while I was at work this morning. I would get pimples every-so-often at the corners of my nostrils. I must have looked stupid to the nameless girl. I rolled my sleeves up and turned the water on.

I ran some water over my face and hair and stared into the sink. The pristine white sink sparked an old word of faith in my life— order. Order was something I had always known, but was losing over the more recent years. Order always gave me a sense that things will work themselves out as long as I did the things I was told and others did the same. The clean sink renewed that faith just enough. It always amazed me how the little things here could change one's state of mind. I grabbed a paper towel and dried my hands and face. My dark eyes seemed to grow a bit lighter. I smiled at myself in the mirror as I took one last look into my eyes; I tightened my tie back up, and made my way back behind the counter.

After about ten minutes of pretending to look busy, I decided to sit down in one of the booths. Like always, between breakfast and lunch, we had no customers. Only Amy's friend and brother were in the café. I sat close enough to eavesdrop. One thing that was interesting about the job was listening to all the things that the kids would talk about. Living vicariously through these kids was a way for me to gain experiences I never had.

"So who is this guy?" I overheard Amy's nameless friend ask.

"He's the guy from next door. He has the most amazing eyes. The deepest blue I have ever seen," Amy replied.

"What's his name?"

"Magnus."

"That's kind of a strange name," Amy's brother stated.

"Yeah, well he's a strange guy. But, I like that. I have never met a guy that is so good-looking, but seems so awkward and clumsy around people. Most of the good-looking guys are overly confident and annoying. I like that he is different."

I kept trying to crane my neck to see over the booth and get a glimpse of Amy's nameless friend. I think she may have noticed me. Their conversation changed from talking about the guy from next door to stuff about what they were going to be doing on the upcoming weekend. She was very animated when she talked and she smiled a lot. Watching her talk was amazing.

How could I get into the conversation? I never knew how. I sat, listened, and waited for opportunities that, if presented to me, I would be too stupid to pick up on and miss, anyway. Where I was from, no one ever listened to me. I was the lowest wrung on the ladder, so to speak. I developed anti-social behavior very early on in my life. I was part of the "do as your told" crowd. I kept my head down and did just that for a large portion of my life. My time here, though, started to peel that shell away bit by bit. I still lacked many social skills.

I smiled when I heard her say something appealing. She knew I was listening. They always knew. *How could I get to know her?* Eavesdropping seemed so conniving and adolescent, but I did it anyway. In this way I learned as much as I could through as little social interaction as possible.

"Bye, it was nice meeting you," the nameless beauty said with a smile.

"It was nice meeting yous, as well," I said "yous," to not look like I only cared to say it to her.

Gone. Another day came to a close at the coffeehouse.

On my way home, she was all I could think about. It was probably more dangerous than driving drunk. I was driving under the influence of lust. I should have been arrested. The highway was barren, like it always was. No one drove east after ten. I left the green fire of the café, only to drive through the green fire of the world's forests. Even at night, the fire burned bright—burning over a backdrop of nighttime shadows—her face stared out of the fire. Her hair burst into the night sky with an auburn glow. It flickered and crackled as it made its way to the edge of the atmosphere.

Her image was drilled into my brain, burning my vision along with the fire of the leaves. She was breathtaking. I knew I would remember her forever.

I had to talk to someone. I had to find out if what I was feeling was normal. I had never been infatuated with any person like this. The fires were burning brighter than ever. I reached into my pocket and pulled out my cell phone. I only had one number stored in my phone's memory.

"This is Aggie." The man's voice on the other end was the only familiar voice I could remember. His grizzled voice had in it the roughness of a military leader and the wisdom of age.

"Hello, Aggie. It's Sam."

"It's been awhile, Sam."

"Yes it has."

"Are you calling about the search?"

"No. I wanted to ask you a question."

Aggie had always been there for me. He was my friend, my mentor, and my brother.

"What is it?" asked Aggie.

"I see the fire everywhere now. The wallpaper at work turns into fire, the forests on the drive to and from work turn into fire, and in my dreams, and…" I paused, "…this girl. I can't get her out of my head."

"Hmm, very interesting. Well, after awhile we all see fire. I…"

I interrupted him, "When did you start seeing it?"

He answered quickly, "When I was younger."

"Does it stop?" I asked.

"It should, eventually. It's been so long, actually, I don't remember that much about it."

"Could it have something to do with love?"

"It could be, I guess. I never fell in love…" Aggie trailed off. I thought I heard a soft "hmm" as if he were thinking of something.

"What is it?" I asked.

He paused before continuing. "I'll see you this weekend," he said with a very curious intonation.

"You don't need to come all the way here. What's going on? What are you thinking?"

"I'll tell you this weekend."

"Uh, okay," I said confusingly.

"I have to think about this a bit."

"Uh, okay," I said again. I don't think he was even paying attention to me anymore.

"I'll see you this weekend. Bye for now," he said abruptly.

"Bye for now," I replied and hung up the phone.

I'm not sure that calling him helped me at all. At any rate, I had made it home during the phone call. I was tired. I got undressed and slipped under the covers. I laid on my bed for what felt like hours, staring at the ceiling, thinking about the fires, the girl, and my conversation with Aggie.

Then, like every night, I went to sleep and dreamt…alone.

My dreams were haunted with uneasiness. Alone in a sea of chaos, I flew. Like a god, I floated over the entire earth, or at least my known world, and observed every aspect of life. I had no power to manipulate the surroundings. I had no power to help the struggling. I had no power to interact. No beautiful women in my dreams…no pain, either. I dreamt, with only the power to see it all. I have always seen all the angles. I have seen all of the sides to all of the stories…except my own. *Does someone who only knows how to follow orders even have a story?*

The only recognizable part of my dreams, were the fires. I guess staring at burning green images all day long while awake, translated into red flames in my dreams. The flames shot up all around me, like red banana leaves and autumn forests. I traveled over the highways and metropolitan cities. I saw all of the injustices that are occurring every day in every way. I looked upon desolation and realized that each human life is quite insignificant. I tried to remember why I was even here. I had always felt that I was here for some greater purpose.

My waking world was never clearer after having those dreams. If anything, the dreams made me feel less significant. When some people dream, they'd get answers. When I would dream, I'd get questions.

Chapter 3
Amy

"Coffee, black and hot."

"Good morning, Magnus."

I looked at the girl behind the counter. It was not the same girl from the day before. That girl had brown hair and brown eyes. The girl behind the counter was a blonde. Blonde, with blue eyes. I got a read on her. She looked innocent and was just being nice. I stared at her blankly while she got my coffee. I had been in the coffee house a thousand times and never bothered to think twice about the servers. They normally would leave my memory as quickly as they would enter it. But that was no longer the case. These girls were being nice to me, and calling me by my name. No one ever bothered to do that before. The hint of personal appreciation had changed my morning ritual.

"That's, one ninety-five."

I put the money on the counter and began to turn away. Then something stopped me. I believe it was either curiosity or fear. Whatever the reason, I had to ask her a question.

"How do you know my name?" I asked as I turned to face her.

"Well…" she replied, not expecting my question. "My friend Amy thinks you're cute and she is always talking about you."

"Who is this, Amy?" I questioned, sounding like an interrogator.

"My friend, she was working yesterday," she said quickly, taking a step back from the counter.

"The brunette?" I continued questioning.

"Yeah. Look sir, I didn't mean anything…" she started to say apologetically.

"What does that mean?"

"Well…you seem upset."

"No. Not at all," I said as I lowered my voice and slowed down to a more pleasant tone. "How did Amy know my name?"

"From your name tag at the marketplace next door."

That made a lot of sense. I should have thought of that. She probably had been coming into the store to buy items for the coffeehouse. I did not wear my name badge in the coffee shop, but I did wear it next door.

The manager of the coffeehouse pushed open the saloon doors of the back room and stared at me.

"Thank you," I said and turned away. I needed to leave, immediately. The manager was making me uneasy again. He looked right at me. I had a feeling he was trying to figure out where he knew me.

I walked out the front door and realized I had overlooked a key piece of the conversation: Amy thought I was "cute". I had never been referred to as "cute", and it made me feel strange, somewhat sick.

As I was contemplating the dilemma of being "cute", I walked unexpectedly into a shopping cart from the store. I looked up to see an old woman with several bags of groceries in the cart. The thick glasses she was wearing led me to believe that she never saw me.

"Oh, I'm sorry," she said through her cracked lips. "Did you hurt yourself?"

"No. Do you need help taking these groceries to your car?"

"No. I live around the corner." She pointed down the road.

"You are not taking our shopping cart to your house, are you?"

She stared back at me not saying a word. I knew all too well that she was going to take the cart. She probably had a dozen of them parked on her front lawn. I just shook my head and walked around her. It was not worth my time.

I walked through the automatic doors of the marketplace and saw the cashiers standing around. One had a bottle of window cleaner in her hand, but she was not using it. They were all chewing gum and ignoring the customers. Not a single one had their shirt tucked in.

"Hello, Magnus."

"Hello," I quickly replied as I walked past them.

I could tell they were shocked. I had never said hello to them in the morning. They stared at me and looked dumbfounded on what to do next. I surely was not going to have small talk with them, so I quickly walked to the back of the store.

It was a truck day, and that meant a lot of work needed to be done. The product that the truck had brought in would have to be taken off the pallets and stocked throughout the store. It was not difficult work, but it was time consuming, and the stockers always seemed to mess it up. They never seemed to know where things went and were always putting cases of product in the wrong location. Between these mistakes, their goofing-off, and flirting with the cashiers, a truck day would always be a hectic one. The back room was a disaster. Pallets of product were piled high in the back room. Half of them were knocked over and two stockers were sitting on boxes eating potato chips.

"Hey, what's up?" one of the stock boys asked, jumping up and pretending to look busy.

I turned around, left the back room, and walked to the front of the store. I did not want to deal with the mess they had made. I was tired of doing all their work. This time, they would have to figure out a way through their incompetence on their own. I just wanted to evaluate the Amy situation and what I was going to do next.

As I got to the front of the store, the cashiers were staring at me. I took out my keys, opened the door to the front office, and locked the door behind me after I went inside. The office was small and always reeked of bad coffee. The assistant manager always left his half-empty cups of coffee lying around, and that day was no different. I threw a half dozen Styrofoam cups in the garbage and sat down at the desk. It was a cheap Formica desk that had a computer and a phone. Underneath the desk was the safe. That was about all the contents of the office.

I looked up the coffeehouse in our customer directory. The telephone number was on file. I picked up the phone and quickly dialed the number.

"Thanks for calling—"

"Yes, is…" I rudely interrupted the person on the other line. "Is…is…is the blonde working?"

In my rush to leave the café in the morning, I never got her name.

"What?" he asked, sounding confused.

"I was in the store earlier and a girl behind the counter with yellow hair was helping me. I must speak to her."

"Jess. Phone call," the kid yelled.

"Hi, this is Jessica," a girl's voice answered.

"I was in your store earlier and was talking to you about your friend."

"Is this Magnus?"

"Yes."

"I'm really sorry about this morning, I didn't mean anything…"

"It is alright. I just wanted to ask you a few questions."

"Okay," she replied.

"Magnus to the front!" blared over the store intercom.

"Your friend Amy…"

"Yeah…"

"Well, is she…" I trailed off trying to figure out the correct words to say.

"Is she what?"

"Never mind."

"Do you want to know if she is available?" she asked teasingly.

"I believe so," I said quietly

"You believe she is available?"

"No, I believe I am asking if she *is* available."

"Oh," she said sounding confused. "Well, she's not seeing anyone."

"Do you think she would—"

"Magnus to the front!" once again blared over the store intercom. "I have to go. I will call you back in a few minutes."

"Okay," she replied and hung up the phone.

I opened the door and stormed out of the office. Two of the cashiers were standing around. The third was helping a customer at the register.

The fattest of three cashiers pointed at a customer standing at the front counter. "That guy is looking for…what are you looking for?" she asked rudely, nearly spitting out her gum.

"I need a coffee maker," the heavy, balding, white man at the counter responded.

"Did you see the one we have in aisle six?" I asked.

"Your cashier told me you don't carry them in the store and I had to order it."

"No. We have it. Follow me, I will show you."

I walked toward aisle six in disgust. None of the employees could ever take the time to learn what we actually carried in stock. I had no idea how this place would stay in business if it were not for me.

"This is it," I told the customer pointing to the coffee machine.

"No, that isn't it," he replied, looking at the price.

"Did you have something special in mind?" I asked politely.

"The coffee pot I have looks different than this one."

"It may be a different model than the one you currently have. But I can assure you, it does make coffee," I said sarcastically.

25

"Hey, pal, I see no reason to be a smart ass."

"I did not mean to offend you."

"Well, you did."

"Sorry."

"You know, these things are not cheap. I want to make sure I am getting what I want. Did that ever occur to you?"

"Did it ever occur to you, that perhaps you do not want the same machine you currently have since the one you have broke? Or perhaps we do not carry that model because they stopped making it twenty years ago?"

He stared at me blankly before turning around and leaving. It amazed me that the stock boys and cashiers can be incredibly rude, but as soon as I make an honest suggestion to the customer he would get upset.

I had little time to worry of this. I needed to get back to the office and call…Amy's friend. I could not believe that I had forgotten the girl's name that quickly.

I hoped I would remember it while I was walking back to the office. *Was it Jenny? Julie?* No, those were not right. I walked into the office, picked up the phone, and dialed the number to the coffeehouse.

"Thanks for calling—"

"Can I talk to the blonde?"

"Jess, it's for you!" the kid yelled.

Jess. Of course, Jessica was her name.

"Hi, this is Jessica."

"Hello, this is Magnus again. We were just talking about your friend Amy."

"Yes," she said with a laugh, "I remember."

"Magnus to the front!" blared over the store intercom.

"This is getting ridiculous."

"Excuse me?" she asked.

"Nothing. Sorry. Just work. I will call you back in a few minutes. I am sorry."

She hung up without saying anything. I could tell she was growing bored and probably annoyed of me. I got up quickly from the desk and opened the office door. All three cashiers were standing around doing nothing.

"What?" I asked the three of them, as I grew impatient.

"Nothing," the oldest one said. "We took care of it."

"Amazing," I retorted, and returned to the office.

As I sat down at the desk I realized I was getting upset. Something I seldom did. In fact, I could not remember the last time I had gotten upset. Something was bringing my emotions to a boil. I did not know if it was the incompetence of the cashier's, the idiocy of the customers, or the task of trying to find out more about Amy, but something had gotten to me.

I tried to regain my composure and once again called the number for the coffeehouse.

"Thanks for calling—"

"Can I talk to Jessica?"

"Jess, it's your boyfriend!" the kid yelled, teasingly.

"Look, you can't keep calling me," she said as she answered the phone. "My boss is starting to get pissed."

"I am sorry," I said as I gathered my courage. I knew this was my chance to ask. "Do you know if she would like to go out with me sometime?"

"I think so. She did say you were cute."

"Great. Do you have her phone number so I can call her?"

"Well, she just showed up to pick up her check."

"She is at the coffeehouse?"

"Yeah. Hey Amy, Magnus is on the phone," she teased her friend. "He wants to know if you want to go out some time?" she asked Amy, pausing to hear her response.

I could hear Amy asking for the phone. But it seemed like Jessica was having too much fun teasing her to give her the phone.

"When?" Jessica asked me.

"How about tonight?"

"He wants to go tonight," she told Amy. She paused again to hear her response. I really would have liked for her to have given the phone to Amy. "She can't tonight, how about tomorrow?" she asked.

"Tomorrow is fine," I replied.

"She says to meet her in the coffeehouse tomorrow at eight."

"I will."

"Bye," she said hanging up the phone.

I hung up the phone and realized I was breathing heavily. I had never done anything like that before. For the first time I could remember, I felt alive. I had finally bridged the gap that I never thought I would. I overcame the fear of this woman. I was so close to realizing whether I made the right choice. A choice I had made long ago, and questioned every day. It was then that I realized that the coffeehouse manager would likely be at the café when I go to meet Amy. He always was. It did not matter, I had to see her, and nothing was going to stop me. All I had to do was figure out what we were going to do.

Chapter 4
Jessica

"Can you tell that guy to stop calling?" I asked Jessica, as she hung up the phone.

"He likes Amy," Jessica yelled across the café. The door was closing behind Amy as she left after picking her check up.

"We have work to do. We need to figure out what is going on for this Thursday," I said, motioning for Jessica and the two other employees working, to sit down in the booth with me. No customers, of course, so I figured that we had plenty of time. I commanded the straggling employees, "Come on."

The three employees took seats in the booth with me. My papers were scattered all over the table. The employees must have taken my neat stacks of notes, looked at them, and threw them uncaringly back onto the table earlier today. The owners only gave me three weeks to prepare for the open mic night. We already had the stage, stool, and mic, but I was still unsure of how to actually promote and run the event.

"So, you know that guy from next door? The one that comes in every day and orders a large coffee?" Jessica asked, not waiting for an answer, "Magnus? Well, he really likes Amy."

"Jessica, can we take care of this?" I made a pitiful attempt to stay focused.

"Yes, boss," she said with a smirk.

"Okay, thank you. Alright, how have your efforts been so far in letting the kids at your schools know about the open mic night?" I asked.

"Well, I told everyone in all of my classes," one of the kids replied, scoffing at Jessica.

"Me too," the other kid said.

"Jessica?" I prodded her.

"Huh?" she shrugged me off.

"Did you tell everyone at your school about Thursday, Jessica?" I asked, again. I watched her eyes look through me. I heard the bell sound at the door as someone entered. Customers seemed to show up as soon as I sat down. I signaled for the kid on the end of the booth to take care of the customer. I turned my attention back to Jessica.

"Oh yeah, well, I kinda forgot," Jessica said. She blushed and curled her hair between her fingers.

I put on the act of being disappointed. I think most of my actions were merely a series of past behaviors I have witnessed, displayed at what I felt were appropriate moments. I stared at her for a few seconds.

She couldn't hold back her smile. "Just kidding, boss," Jessica said, reverting back to a straight face with little success.

I reorganized the papers on the table. I nodded to the customer, who got his coffee and headed out of the store. "Just pay attention from behind the counter," I told the worker who assisted the customer. I went back to reorganizing the papers. Sometimes, making order out of chaos helps us find what it is we are looking for. "Sometimes…"

Jessica interrupted, "I thought it was going to be that guy from next door. Wouldn't that be weird? I mean…I was just talking about him and then…"

"Jessica, can we get back to Thursday?" She made me forget what I was originally going to say. That seemed to happen often with her. "How about this? After we finish discussing what we are going to do for Thursday, you can gossip all you want about Amy, the guy next door, love, music, cars, Amy's friend, relationships, the mall, or whatever you can imagine? How does that sound?" I pleaded. Jessica had a way to get me off track.

"Sounds good, boss," Jessica said, folding her arms onto the tabletop. She leaned in at attention.

"Okay, I need someone to host this thing. Any ideas of who it should be, or volunteers?" I asked, not wanting to be the host.

"I think Jessica should do it," the worker behind the counter piped up. "She likes to be the center of attention."

"Shut up. I do not," she shook her head as she disagreed.

"I'm not sure we would be able to get her off the mic," the other worker chided.

"Shut up."

"Okay now, leave her alone," I said. I don't know why I came to her defense. "If she doesn't want to do it, I understand."

"Thank you, boss."

For some reason, every time she called me boss, I felt empowered, and in a way respected. This job was the first time I had ever been in charge of anyone or anything. "You're welcome, Jessica. Now who is going to…"

The door chimed, again. Another customer came in.

"What time is it?" I asked Jessica.

"It's almost five, boss," answered Jessica.

"Well, I guess we'll have to do this tomorrow." We would often get busy around five—not always, but often enough to where we needed to be ready. I got up from the booth and headed behind the counter. Jessica followed, as did the other employee. They checked the coffees and snacks to make sure everything was made or stocked. I trained them well. I was going home soon.

"So, this guy, Magnus, he is kinda weird," Jessica started gossiping.

"Jessica, not around customers," I whispered to her.

"What about you, boss, any girl in your life?"

"No."

"That's sad. Why not?" Jessica inquired.

"No time," I answered. "Come on, we need to get ready."

"I can talk and work at the same time."

"I know you can. Anyway, I have to go soon," I added. "You can gossip tomorrow, since it seems I'm not going to get much help with this open mic night. I guess I will have to be host."

"I think you'll make a great host, boss," said Jessica.

"Thank you, Jessica," I replied. I then raised my voice so the other employees could hear. "Can all of you help me out by at least reading some poetry or something on Thursday? Or, maybe, bring people who will participate?"

"We'll do what we can, boss."

The next day, Jessica, Amy, and I were scheduled to close. I figured I wouldn't be able to get through the door without them talking about the guy next door who liked Amy. *Who knew how many times that guy had called while I was gone?* I don't know why I even cared.

When I got to work, the morning employees were just about to leave and Jessica was the only employee remaining. Amy had not come in yet.

"Where is Amy today?" I asked.

"She called into work today. I'm not sure why," Jessica said.

"Is someone coming to work her shift?"

"Not that we know of. It's just you and me, boss," Jessica replied with a smile.

Without skipping a beat I asked the leaving workers for a favor, "Can you guys stick around for a little bit to make sure that things are a bit more tidy before you leave? That way, the two of us aren't swamped too badly."

"No problem," the two of them replied.

"I think she is embarrassed or something," Jessica added.

I thought to myself, "When will it end." I shrugged off Jessica's comments and went to the back room. I hung up my jacket and took a seat at the desk. Flipping on the computer, I got up to make myself a cup of tea. I liked that the tea was free. Most jobs don't have such benefits. Most companies will provide medical, dental, and optical insurance, but I just wanted tea. Those other jobs seemed like a lot of hard work for very little pay off. Anyway, I was not here to do those things. Grander objectives were controlling my destiny.

I made a cup of red tea and sat back down at my desk. I always drank red tea. Before I worked at the coffeehouse, I had to import it to wherever I was living. It used to be so hard to find. You could get green tea anywhere. I never liked green tea. Drinking red tea was a much more fulfilling experience. The tastes of the red tea leaves, with twists of citrus or flowers, were pleasant to me. The aromas of various kinds of red teas gave me a sense that the world was vulnerable; even the most beautiful creations of Earth are reaped by mankind for their personal tastes and desires. Nothing is sacred here.

"We cleaned up and we're leaving," the two morning employees said from the front of the café.

I got up to say goodbye. They were already gone by the time I made it out of the back room. I had told my employees that I didn't care much for simple pleasantries. Although, I would constantly make an effort to say my "Hellos" and "Goodbyes." I felt so out of place that I did anything to blend in.

I looked out front and only Jessica was left. I knew it was time for the gossip. I didn't mind so much, I guess. Jessica was an attractive girl, so, it wasn't too hard to watch and listen to her speak. Where I am from, the females are kind of hard to look at, which makes it somewhat difficult to remain focused on their words. Plus, they were generally barking orders at me, so I would hear what I needed to and ignore the rest. That wasn't the case here.

Figuring I would start the inevitable ball rolling, I began, "So, Amy and this guy from next door…"

"Oh yeah, I totally forgot…"

"Yeah, right," I interrupted.

"About that," she continued, "well, actually, Amy is the one who started liking him first. I kinda let the cat out of the bag, though, and told him. Ever since, he has been calling. He is cute, but he seems kinda strange. Especially the way he reacts to everything."

"What do you mean?" I inquired.

"Well, he was all weirded out that I knew his name. I mean, duh, it's on his name badge when I go next door. And he reacted even more weird when I told him that Amy thought he was cute. I think that is why she called in sick today. I told her that he keeps calling. I don't know what she is so creeped out about, *she* is the one who likes *him*," Jessica said, all in one breath. I knew she was covering for Amy, though. I let it slide.

"I'm calling her to tell her to come to work," I said. I wasn't angry, I was just curious about this whole thing. The guy seemed uneasy when I had come out of the back room the other day after he had gotten his coffee. I never did anything to him. It just seemed like odd behavior. Although, the more people I met, the stranger and stranger they would be. "She'll come in."

"Are you going to play matchmaker or something, boss?" Jessica asked.

"No, I just think we need one more person tonight to close."

"Well, don't tell her that I told you anything," pleaded Jessica.

"I won't. I don't do things like that," I assured her.

I picked up the phone and dialed. Amy answered after only one ring.

"Hello, Amy, this is Samuel, your boss," I said. "Were you expecting someone else?"

"Oh, hi, I…" Amy stuttered, "I can't come into work today."

"I figured that much out," I said. "Why didn't you call me, though? You know the rules." I knew Amy had a hard time lying to me.

"Well, I have a date tonight."

"With that guy from next door?"

"Yes. I meant to call you, because," she paused, "we are actually meeting at the coffeehouse. Is that okay?" She sounded like she was embarrassed.

"I guess." The fact was, I didn't care. I just wanted her to tell me the truth. That is all I ever asked of my employees. Jessica was different when it came to this. We had a different relationship where I knew what she was up to so it never really mattered what she actually said. "I'll tell you what, if you bring your friend to the open mic night, I will look passed this."

"My date?" Amy asked.

"No, no. Your friend from the other day that came in with your brother," I added.

"Oh, Sarah? Okay. Deal. She was going to come anyway. It is a little awkward, though, because she just broke up with my brother. It's a long story, though," she said.

"Well, I am sure you will tell me about it next time you work." All the girls at work would tell me their life stories, their families' life stories, and their friends' life stories. It always amazed me how many things happen in one person's life. "I guess we'll see you soon."

"See you soon," she added as she hung up the phone.

Chapter 5
Magnus and Amy

"Coffee, black and hot."

"Hi, Magnus."

"Hello, *Jessica*." I added emphasis when I said her name. It bothered me that I had forgotten her name. She gave me a funny look as I said it. It was probably because it was not her that was on the phone when I forgot her name. She likely knew nothing of it.

"Amy hasn't shown up yet. She's probably still getting ready."

"That is fine."

"You can have a seat while you wait."

"Thank you."

I sat down at one of the tables near the counter. A small stage with a microphone and a stool was set up over in the corner where a table was the day before.

"What is that?" I asked Jessica, pointing to the stage.

"The microphone? We are having an open mic night tomorrow. You should come by."

"What for?"

"Because it'll be fun."

"Not, 'what should I come for?' I am wondering what is the open mic for?"

"It's for people to get up and read poems and sing songs. You know, kind of a way to express yourself."

I nodded knowing full well what it was. It was an obvious marketing gimmick to bring more people in. Self-loathing people that get upset that no one ever bothers to listen to them. They get up on stage and rant about how depressing their life is. No one listens. Everyone is too busy in his or her own self-loathing to bother. I knew I would not be going.

I was lost in the thought of the pathetic people that would be in the coffeehouse for the event, when the door chimed and Amy walked in. Up to that moment I had only seen her wearing her work uniform. She always wore her black hat and black apron with her hair drawn back in a tail. Today she wore a tight pair of jeans and a bright red sweater. Her long, brown hair was slightly curled and bounced around her shoulders ever so softly. Her make-up showed the innocence of her brown eyes. I finally got a read on her. She was radiant. I could not take my eyes off her. I was staring into a fire whose flickering beauty consumed my very being.

"Hi, Magnus. Are you ready?"

I snapped back to reality and brought myself together as I tried to get my brain to start working again. "Sure," I replied. I was no longer staring into the fire, but I could still feel its heat. I could feel her heat. A heat I had never felt before. Something magical was happening. The heat was a welcome comfort to me, and for the first time ever I was not nervous to be around another. I knew, no matter what happened that night, that the decision I made was the correct one.

"Do you have anything in mind?"

"Not really."

"Ohh…"

"How about a movie?" I blurted. It was the first thing I thought of. It seemed she did not like the fact that I had nothing planned. I often heard the stock boys at the store asking the cashiers to go to the movies. This seemed as good as option as any.

"That's fine," she replied. It seemed that it was not the option she had in mind.

"We can do something else if you like."

"No, no. A movie sounds great. I really want to see that one with..."

I was not listening anymore. I was staring into her eyes. I was back staring into the fire. It was a fire like none other. The orange and red flames that I knew all too well were dancing around a stronger, hotter, and more beautiful flame of clear blue that I had never seen before. The orange and red flames danced around the blue in honor of its beauty.

Amy was still talking. I was still not listening. She turned and walked toward the front door. She continued to talk to my deaf ears. I was thoroughly entranced. This creature had cast a spell, and I was enthralled. It was not until we walked outside, and the cool, night air hit my face, that I came back to reality. The cool air was like a slap across my face for me to pay attention to her.

"Let's go to the old theatre across the street? That way we don't have to drive."

"Sure," I said. Her voice was beautiful.

I could tell by her expression that her smile was beginning to fade and she was growing impatient. I must have seemed difficult to her. She was asking me questions, and I was barely paying attention. I needed to make this date fun for her. It was just a girl. I needed to regain my composure. *What was she talking about?* It was time to think. She looks cold. We were going to a movie. She said to go across the street. Wait, she was already on the move. She was about twenty feet away in the parking lot.

"Are you coming?" she asked with an impatient laugh.

"Yes, I am sorry. Just a little lost in thought."

"You're a strange one." The smile was back on her face, and it was amazing. She must have been enjoying my presence. I quickened my step to catch up to her.

"What theatre are we going to?"

"The one across the street. I think the movie is starting soon."

We walked across the parking lot of the plaza that the marketplace and coffeehouse were a part of. It was a cool, damp night and the parking lot was dark with the asphalt being slightly wet. It was cool out, but not cold. Several of our store's shopping carts were straggled throughout the lot. I realized I left work without caring. I was in such a rush to meet Amy that I never checked if everything was done.

We got to the intersection and the crosswalk light looked as if it were about to change. Amy did not want to wait. She grabbed my hand as she half-walked, half-ran across the street trying to beat the traffic. She dragged me along like I was a child crossing the street for the first time.

"It's playing," she yelled to me as she looked at the marquis for the movie theatre.

"Great," I added, trying to seem thrilled as I awkwardly ran after her. I looked up at the marquis to see what she was looking at. I do not know why I bothered; I knew I would not know any of the movies playing. I did not know which one she wanted to see.

She let go of my hand when we reached the other side of the street. It was at this time that I realized she had been touching me. I stopped on the sidewalk just outside the movie theatre. She had no fear of me. No fear at all. All this time, I had thought that women were afraid of me. I was wrong. I was afraid of them.

She ran behind me and pushed me in the lower back. "C'mon, it's probably starting soon."

She touched me again. I did not need to look into the fire. It had consumed me.

We walked into the theatre. Amy told the clerk what movie we wanted to see.

"That will be eighteen dollars."

I looked at the clerk in amazement. It seemed a little expensive. I did not want to seem strange though. I quickly pulled out my money clip and put the money on the counter.

"Thanks. It's showing in theatre two. Enjoy the show."

"Thanks. You too," Amy replied.

We walked down the carpeted hallway that led to theatre two. Her reply to the clerk had confused me. She said 'you too' which made no sense to me since the clerk was not seeing the movie. I did not have any more time to think about it, since we were walking up to the door of the theatre. Amy swung the door open and waited for me to catch it before she walked into the dark theatre.

"I like to sit close so I don't have to wear my glasses. Is that okay?"

"Sure, wherever you like." It was my first time in a movie theatre and I had no idea where the best place was to sit. I knew my best chance of making this an enjoyable evening for her was to fake my way through it and let her make as many of the decisions as possible.

"This looks good," she said, pointing to a couple of seats near the aisle way.

We sat down and watched the movie. I could not have cared less about what was playing. It was an animated film about a fish. It was quite boring to me. I never liked the sea, and this movie did nothing to change my view. I just sat and enjoyed Amy's company. It was the first night I had ever spent alone with another, and I was enjoying it.

I tried a few times to pay attention to the movie. My attempts were futile. The story was of no interest to me, and my eyes would roam from the screen to Amy. The light from the projection screen gave just enough light to show the beauty of her face. A few times when I looked over, she looked back at me, and we stared into each other's eyes. It was as if we were talking without saying a word. She would then turn away and watch the screen again. She seemed to have enjoyed the movie since she laughed and smiled throughout the entire film. I wish I could have enjoyed it along with her. When the movie ended, we got up and walked out of the theatre. The credits were still playing and the music was loud. She looked like she wanted to say something, but she knew that I would not be able to hear her.

As we made our way down the hallway she turned to me and asked, "So what did you think?"

"It was good."

"Really, you didn't laugh at all. Or even smile."

"It was not my kind of movie."

"You more of an action guy?"

"Probably."

"You're not much of a talker either?"

"Excuse me?"

"Nothing, don't take it the wrong way. I was just saying...never mind."

"No, please, continue."

"Well, it just seems that you like to say only what is needed. And then, it's usually in such a direct way, that...I don't know."

"I am sorry."

"See, that's what I am saying. You seem so rigid and tense. You talk like you're on an interview, or on trial or something. Lighten up, tell me a little bit about yourself."

"What do you need to know?"

"I don't *need* to know anything, Magnus. It is what you *want* me to know. Tell me about your family, where you come from, what your favorite foods are, or some story of when you were younger. You know, the stuff you talk about on a date."

"I am sorry. I have very little to tell about those things," I said, looking deep into her eyes. The fire was beginning to fade away.

"I kinda figured that," she said with a shrug. "Well, thanks for going anyway. And, hey, thanks for paying."

41

I nodded my head to her to let her know that it was not a problem as I opened the door for her. We walked out of the theatre and were once again standing in the cold night.

"I should probably get going home," she said looking down the street, sounding somewhat bored of the evening.

"I never knew my parents and I have no siblings. I have some distant cousins that I never talk to. I moved here years ago. I like spicy foods and I cannot stand ice cream. The only people I ever knew sent me away when I was young to study abroad."

"Wow. That was a lot," she said, amazed.

"Sorry," I replied quietly.

"No need to be sorry, in fact, stop saying you're sorry."

"Yes."

"Good," she said then paused. "You said that you were sent away to study?"

"Yes."

"Where at?"

"Mainly Europe."

"Wow, that must have been an experience," she added. She sounded quite interested. "What did you study?"

I hesitated for a moment. No one had ever asked me any of these questions, and certainly no one knew any of this about me. "Mainly sociology and psychology," I continued.

"That is really interesting. If you went to school studying in Europe, how come you work at a grocery store?"

"It was my old job that had me go for the schooling. I did not like it, so I quit."

"What didn't you like, the school or the job?"

"Both, but mainly the job."

"What didn't you like about it?"

"Pretty much everything." She could tell I was growing uncomfortable talking about my past. "It was a job that I was expected to do. Many from where I come, worked very hard to make sure I had the best education and training possible. After awhile, I realized the job was not for me and I needed to make a change."

"Well, people change jobs all the time. You just need to do what makes you happy, I guess."

"I believe that is what I am doing."

"Well…that makes one of us," she said looking up at the night sky.

"You are not happy?"

"I'm happy. I'm just not happy doing what I'm doing."

"What do you mean? You are not happy at the coffeehouse?"

"Kinda," she said, shrugging her shoulders. "I always thought I'd do more; that I would be more. I always wanted to change the world. But the older I get, the more I realize that it'll never happen."

"Why do you think that?"

"No one can change the world, Magnus. We will still have rich people, poor people, mean people, nice people. Nothing ever changes. At least nothing that I can do."

"I think you may be looking at this the incorrect way."

"What do you mean? You think one person can change the world?" she asked.

"I know one person can change the world. It is just a matter of what you think change is."

"Well…" she said, growing confused.

"I mean, I do not think one person can end poverty, or world hunger, or war, at least not over night. But I know one person's actions can have a great deal of influence on the entire world."

"Who?"

"Who, what?"

"Who? Back up your argument, Mr. College-Education," she said teasingly.

"Sorry, I was just talking."

"No, no. I want to know.

"Okay, well, for one, the Archduke Ferdinand."

"Who's that?"

"Well, he was a very well known member of the church in the early nineteen-hundreds. His assassination is what triggered all of Europe into World War I."

"I don't think that counts."

"Why not?"

"It is nothing he did. It was what someone else did. You know, the person who killed him."

"Nonetheless, whether it was him or the one who killed him, one person changed the world forever."

"I guess," she said, sounding as if I was a salesman trying to snag her. "That's a stretch though. You got another?"

"I think Adolf Hitler, as well, would qualify. It was his will and tyranny that drove Germany into the war machine that would change the world forever."

"I don't think that one counts either. You keep talking about how people are changing the world for the worse."

"Well, it seems throughout human history it has always been easier to destroy than create. I believe it has something to do with the creation of chaos and the lack of order. I believe the second law of thermodynamics explains it."

"What?" she asked confusingly.

"Nothing, I was babbling."

"You still haven't given me anyone who changed the world for the better?"

"I think one could debate for the rest of eternity if the world ended up better or worse after each of the world wars. But, I do not think that debate is what you are looking for."

"You weren't kidding about going to school."

"Sorry?"

"Sure you weren't a philosophy major?" she said with a laugh.

"I took some courses in that, too."

"I can tell," she said laughing.

It was good to see her laugh. It was unlike anything I had felt before. I was rambling on about theories and facts of things I had kept inside for years. Not only was I telling someone, but also, that someone was listening.

"Perhaps I should have become a philosopher?" I said, jokingly.

"I don't know, are you any good as a food store manager?"

"It matters who you ask."

She bit her lower lip and stared at me. I think she was trying to tell me something with the silence. I tried to read her eyes, but I could not understand. She was looking at me with an emotion that I did not recognize.

"You still haven't answered my question?" she asked, breaking the uneasy silence.

"I believe I have."

"Not with someone that changed the world for the better."

"Well, I do have one more," I said slowly. I was somewhat uncomfortable talking about this with her. It did not seem like the type of conversation that people have on a date.

"Who?" Her inquiry insured me that she was still interested.

"John Kennedy."

"What, when he got killed?" she asked sarcastically.

"No, before that. John Kennedy was president when a fleet of Soviet shipping vessels began arriving throughout the year of nineteen sixty-two in the communist country of Cuba."

"Yeah, I remember that from class."

"Well, it was believed that those boats carried powerful nuclear weapons with the sole intention of launching an attack on The United States. Both sides of the conflict became very concerned about who knew what, and where each country's missiles were. The situation became known as the 'Cuban Missile Crisis'."

"I think my dad was in the service during it. I still don't see what this has to do with one person changing the world."

"Nothing happened. No weapons were ever fired. To this day, no one knows why President Kennedy backed down, but for the good of the world he did. If he did not, the entire world would have been devastated by the nuclear war that would have ensued. Thus, one person, and his reaction to a situation, changed the world for the better."

She stood quiet and stared at me. She looked a little confused. Like she was not expecting me to go into that deep of an example.

She opened her mouth and paused a second before she spoke, "I'm not sure if that counts either."

"Why not?"

"Because, he didn't *do* anything. If he would've attacked, then that would've changed the world."

"Either way, he changed the world."

"No, the world was still the same. No weapons were used."

"What you are missing is that the weapons were supposed to be used. If the world existed with another in his place, the missiles would have been launched. The world changed with the realization of what the situation was, and a reaction that saved millions of lives.

"You don't know that."

"Perhaps…" I said to her with a smile.

"Anyway," she said with a crooked smile back. "It's getting late. I should get going home."

"Can I walk you to your house?"

"What?"

"Can I walk you to your house? You said you needed to get going home."

"You can walk me to my car if you like? I am parked across the street."

"Sure."

We walked back across the street to the plaza parking lot for the marketplace and coffeehouse. She once again grabbed my hand. This time she did not run. We slowly strolled across the lot.

"It's such a beautiful night," she intervened into our quiet walk across the parking lot.

"I thought it might be a bit cool for you," I replied.

"A bit, but that's the way I like it."

"Why is that?"

"I don't know. I just think it's the way God intended it."

"What do you mean?" I asked with a slight laugh.

"I just think that sunny days are great, and everyone loves a warm day, but nothing is more comfortable than a cool night."

As she was talking, a slight breeze blew her hair around her face. She pulled her hand away from mine to keep her hair out of her face. She was right, it was a cool night, but I would never have known. All I could feel was her warmth, her fire upon my face. She was radiant.

"I would have to agree with you," I replied.

"That it was the way God intended it?"

"No," I replied quietly. "That it is a comfortable night. The most comfortable I can remember."

"I'm sorry. I did not mean to get into…"

"No, it is okay," I told her. I did not want to end our date on an awkward note.

"No, no. I shouldn't have said anything."

"I believe you are overreacting."

"I'm sorry."

"What is the problem?"

"I, just…never mind."

"Something seems to be bothering you."

"It's just…my parents raised me religiously."

"And you are ashamed of that?" I asked with a confused look.

"Well, no. But, it seems like guys don't like to talk about that stuff. In fact, it seems like no one does these days."

"I did not realize we were talking about it. I thought we were talking about the weather."

"We were, but…"

"I know. I was trying to lighten the subject."

"Thanks. Sometimes I can take myself too seriously."

"I understand completely. Often times I wonder what a sense of humor is. And if I will ever get one."

"Well," she said with a laugh. "I think you do."

"Thanks. I think you may be the only one to think so."

"I'm sure others think so. Especially if they get to know how great of a guy you are." she said with a smile as she took my hand again.

"Thanks," I said again. I was starting to like compliments, and was certainly starting to like saying thanks for them.

"Can I ask you something?"

"Of course."

"Do you believe in God?"

I paused. It was a question I was never asked before. I took my time before answering, "It is not a question of belief for me. I know God exists."

"How's that?"

"I have met Him."

"You've met Him?"

"Yes."

"You've met God?"

"Yes."

"How?"

"Have we not all met God somewhere along the way?"

She smiled at me again. "See, that is what I am looking for."

I smiled back at her. She put her arm around mine and laid her head on my shoulder as we continued walking. I was thoroughly enjoying her company, and she seemed quite content with my answer to her question. She never heard me mutter, "I just hope the next time I meet Him goes better."

We walked up to her car and she pulled away from me. The fire faded the further she walked away from me.

"I think I had fun, Magnus."

"I did too."

She unlocked the door to her car and turned to face me. The fire was once again raging before me: the flames, the beauty, and the heat. I welcomed it as she stared into my eyes. She took a small step closer to me.

"Thanks for everything," she said lightly grabbing my tie.

"The pleasure was all mine," I said as she gently tugged on my tie.

"You're not very good with hints are you?"

"Excuse me?"

She gave a quick tug on my tie and my face came close to hers. She put her soft, subtle lips to mine and embraced me. The entire world burst into flames. The warmth of the flames was unbelievable, but the warmth of her kiss was indescribable.

She slowly pulled away from me, and looked into my eyes. I read her thoughts, her emotions, her soul. I saw things in her brown eyes I never thought I would see. She could have seen the same in mine. My defense was finally down. I was completely infatuated with this woman.

"Good night, Magnus," she said as she turned to open the door to her car.

"Can I see you again?" I asked.

"Sure," she said, turning her head slightly to look at me.

"How about tomorrow?"

"I don't know. I might need a day off."

"Sorry."

"I'm just kidding, tomorrow is fine. And quit apologizing" she said as she opened the door to her car.

"Sorr—" I caught myself. "I will," I said to her as she went to sit in her car.

"No, wait," she said before she sat down. "Tomorrow is Thursday. I told my boss that I would be at the open mic night at the café."

"Oh, okay."

"Why don't you come?"

"I wouldn't miss it."

"Great, see you then," she said as she got in her car.

She started the car and waved to me. I stood in the damp parking lot and watched her drive off. I had definitely made the right choice.

Chapter 6
The Open Mic

I was forced to host the open mic night. The coffeehouse started to fill up after the dinner crowd had left. We had put a sign-up sheet at the front of the café so people could put their names down if they wanted to read a poem, perform a song, or whatever else they wanted. The number of people that desired to show their talents surprised me.

I waited until the café was almost full before I went up to the mic. I looked around the room at all the anticipating faces, but I did not see Amy's "nameless" girlfriend. I looked down at the way I was dressed. I wore my red tie—solid red. I had on a white, button-down dress shirt, black pants, and black shoes. As I looked out at the crowd, I realized that I was overdressed for the event. Most of the patrons were wearing jeans, a Polo or T-shirt, or some other type of casual clothing.

The stage was set up simply with a microphone on a stand and a stool. I grabbed a hold of the microphone. Amy and Jessica were sitting in the back of the café together. Jessica was in her work clothes staring right back at me. Amy was dressed nicely. She had mentioned something about meeting the guy from next-door tonight. She was definitely dressed to impress: form-fitting white blouse, top two buttons undone, and tight jeans; still no sign of her "nameless" friend.

"Hello, everyone. Welcome to our first open mic night. From the looks of it, we have quite a few people ready to get on the mic. So, I will shut up and call up the first person." I picked up the list from the table and looked at the first name.

Without reading the name aloud, I looked up from the list at Jessica. She winked at me. "Well, it looks as if someone has written my name down to start things off. I guess I can do that, unless any of yous have any objections?" I waited a few seconds for any replies. I didn't feel embarrassed or nervous. I was just beginning to realize what emotions were. I think that I felt something that could be equated to sorrow, for Jessica. I knew how she felt about me, but it would never be…at least not in this life.

"This poem I wrote…"

Amy's "nameless" friend walked into the café. My eyes followed her, along with my mind, as she walked to the back of the café. My newfound exploration of emotions began with the first time I ever laid eyes on her only a few days prior. I started to notice the things women would do to attract or flirt with men and how couples interacted when they came into the café. I began to understand the mortal struggle between men and women—how it can lift you up to the stars one moment and come crashing down the next. I was a quick learner, too.

"I…I…" Everyone was staring at me. She sat down next to Amy. She was the reason I wrote this poem. "I wrote this yesterday, which is why I have it memorized. Normally I don't have the capacity to remember things like this, but…" I drifted. "Anyway, I call this poem 'Never Forever':

Never Forever

Alone in forever
Gaining never

Chaos insight
Dreams of flight
Looking down
Only a frown
Living is bliss
Always amiss
No more sound
Alone all bound."

During my recital, I noticed the guy from next-door come in, but it didn't distract me from my recital. For some reason, though, when he walked in, it felt that he was precise in his entrance; that he came in exactly when I said the line "Dreams of flight," purposely trying to throw me off. He walked by as I said the words "Chaos insight." Maybe I was just imagining things. *Why would this guy care about interrupting me?*

I had read the poem very methodically, trying to make it more insightful, I guess. I emphasized the key words that I was feeling at that moment: forever, chaos, bliss, always, bound. I tried to look around the room as I was reciting the poem, but I kept looking back to Amy's friend. Her and Amy's attention seemed to be preoccupied with Magnus's entrance. Jessica, however, had her eyes fixed on me the entire time I was on the stage.

I realized that I had been standing up at the microphone for about a minute in silence. A few people had clapped, but most of them, as I could tell, were waiting for me to call the next person up. I looked down at the sheet, then back up to the crowd. "Uh, thank you. Um...next up is a poem by," I had to look down at the sheet again, "Laura Stevenson."

A girl stood up from a booth on the side of the café and walked to the front. She had a very conservative look. She wore a white shirt under an earthy-green knit cardigan. Her brown corduroy pants ended over top of her black dress shoes. The ends of her straight, brunette hair lightly brushed her shoulders.

I made my way to the back of the room where Amy, her "nameless" friend, Jessica, and the guy from next-door were sitting.

"You can sit in my chair, boss," Jessica said. She got up from the table and held the chair out for me. "I guess I have to get back to work anyway."

"I guess so," I said and sat down. "Hello, all."

Jessica shushed me as she walked off, pointing to the girl on the microphone. Everyone at the table whispered "Hello" before the girl up front began her poem. She began, "This poem I wrote, I like to call 'The Song':

At that moment you were the most beautiful song in the world.
I replayed you every day from then on.
Your lyrics inspire me.
Your music moves me through places I have never been before.
You keep taking me to new exciting worlds.
I share you with the world.
Every time I play the song they can see my joy.
The song is from the heart of the earth.
Let your melodic voice melt me.
Beautify and guide me with the song.
The song doesn't change, yet every time I listen I hear something new.
A beat, a word, a chord, an emotion...
I fall in love with you fresh, every day."

I didn't take my eyes from Amy's "nameless" friend throughout the entire poem. She smiled once or twice at me, but mainly she shied away from my stare. At that moment, it was she who was the most beautiful song in the world. I was becoming engulfed with new emotions. For the first time that I could ever remember, someone's words enraptured my senses.

The girl on stage lowered her head and walked back to her seat as everyone politely clapped. She murmured "thank you" a few times before she sat down. Her eyes seemed like they were a little moist. Mine may have been as well.

Amy nudged me, "You have to go back up to the stage," she whispered.

I got up and headed up to the stage. I wondered if I was ever going to get a chance to talk to Amy's "nameless" friend that night. More importantly, I was hoping someone would say her name again. I looked at the list.

"That was a wonderful poem, Laura," I said, looking over to her table. She blushed. "Next up, it looks like James Logan is going to be playing a song. James?"

A skinny, shaggy-haired teen strolled up front holding a guitar. I stepped aside and headed to the back. James flung the guitar strap over his shoulder and grabbed the microphone. "I hope you enjoy this song I wrote. This one is about how the nice guys always finish last. It's called 'Save the Last for the Best.'" He tuned his guitar quickly and began playing a bluesy tune.

He started singing in a very low voice:

"Black and white
Images of late
Clawing at nothing
Hopeless fate.

Crossroads and forks
Pers'nal choice lost

Dead end stares
Feeling the cost.

Save the last,
For the best.

Fear and love
Turn back again
Hands cupped on face
Swallowing the rain.

Save the last,
For the best."

James interrupted the vocals by playing a melodic guitar solo.

"*Found and lost*
Spinnin' in limbo
Ready for more
Readying to go.

Future and past
Representin' choice
The others have gone
Leaving no voice.

Light and dark
Eyes adjust
Step forward
Out of the dust.

Save the last,
For the best."

The café patrons erupted in applause. James took a bow. It seemed to me that he had done this before. He waved a few times as he said his "thank yous" into the microphone. I had no chance to talk to Amy's friend during the song. She looked to be very interested in the music, as was I. I got up and went back to the stage. I shook James's hand and gave him thanks.

"James Logan, ladies and gentlemen. We'll have to give him a night all to himself." I paused a moment to let the applause die down. I took another look at the list. I needed to start talking to Amy's friend. "We'll call a couple more people up, then take a short break before we continue. Next up is Henry Abbott."

Henry Abbott had a lot of hair; brown, curly, almost like an afro. He wore a pair of thick plastic frame glasses and had a pentagon-shaped earring. The jeans and T-shirt he wore looked extra baggy over his bony frame.

I handed him the mic and went back to my seat.

"As we evolve as a species, we add more and more contraptions to our lives. We seem to strive to live in a perfect habitat at all times. This poem is something about that," he started,

The Effects Of Artificial Atmosphere

The effects of the artificial atmosphere
Provide moisture or make the air clear.

Evolve us in the comfort of our lives
At home or work or on to and fro drives.

Make us happy through sunshine and snow
Cool us at a hundred or heat us at zero.

We give artificial atmosphere not just to our own

But animals at zoos or plants that need grown.

Our will be granted to us every day
'Cause to the gods of artificial atmosphere I pray."

Everyone in the café chuckled amidst applause. To me, though, Henry's poem made me think of how ludicrous this world was actually becoming. Looking across the table I felt a mix of emotions. Amy's "nameless" friend looked so beautiful. I caught a bit of the conversation at the table before I was prodded, once again, to get up to the microphone...

Amy turned and said to Magnus, "You should go up and recite a poem or something. I'm sure you're talented." Amy's "nameless" friend nodded her head in agreement.

Magnus replied, "I do not know any poetry."

"Just say something from the heart," Amy encouraged him.

As I made my way to the front, I turned around to see Magnus's reaction to Amy's supporting words. Something about him felt as if he hadn't any heart in him.

Magnus stared her in the eyes and I heard him say, "okay," as I turned back to head up to the stage.

Maybe I was wrong.

"Very interesting outlook, Henry," I paused to look down at the sheet. "Next is Kyle Theissen with a sonnet. After this, we will take a short break. Please feel free to use the restrooms down the hallway in the back, talk amongst yourselves, or buy one of our many flavored coffee beverages or snacks. Also, if you wish to add your name to the list, feel free to do so at the break. Kyle?" I passed Kyle on my way back to my seat.

Kyle had a big smile on his face as he walked to the front. It looked like it was carrying over from his reaction to the poem that was just read, but it had some menace behind it as well. He had on

58

a T-shirt and jeans, just like half of the patrons—in fact, probably half the people on Earth. The T-shirt had some logo on it: maybe a sports team.

I tried to start up a conversation with Amy's "nameless" friend, "I'm sorry, but I forgot your…"

"Hey everyone," Kyle started talking into the mic, "I am sure we have all been in this place before. This poem I wrote, not too long ago, after a pretty harsh break-up. Sometimes it feels really good to get this stuff out. That's why I write. It is basically the first sonnet I ever wrote, so right now it is just called 'Sonnet I':

While I'm tempted to look into your eyes,
I am forc'd to shy away from your gaze.
For I know I will hear the same old lies
That I heard before in the golden days.

O, how I wish one day we could return
To that beautiful meadow we once knew.
In this meadow, the flame of love did burn.
This paradise was created for you.

But bitter, black love doth make it crumble.
And I had thought that you really lov'd me.
How could I have thought that you were humble?
This pure land I will never again see.

Standing in this field, I once had no fears.
But now it is the reason, for my tears."

Being interrupted in my first attempt of the evening to talk to Amy's "nameless" friend threw me into deep concentration. I listened intently to the sonnet. It sparked memories in me that I had long forgotten. Sometime during the sonnet, I drifted into the hissing conflagration of banana leaf wallpaper that writhed behind Amy's "nameless" friend. The flames accentuated her beauty. Something felt very right. I felt, for once in a long time, that I was in the right place, surrounded by this marvel of social interaction. The words that came through the speaker touched me.

"Wow," I slipped.

The sonnet showed me that, once upon a time I was actually able to think for myself. It seemed, recently, that I was merely becoming a slave to a group of bosses using me because of my devotion to duty and the order of things.

I stared into the eyes of Amy's "nameless" friend. "I am really sorry to ask you this, but I forgot what your name is."

"That's okay," she began, "you seemed a little spaced out the first time we met. It's Sarah."

"Thank you, Sarah. I won't forget again. Truth be known, I was so taken by your beauty, that I think I went deaf for a bit at our first meeting." I don't know where those words came from, but I said them.

"Wow," she blushed. Her red face overpowered the flaming banana leaves, bringing them back to their original state. The conflagration had ended.

"You are more powerful than fire," I whispered to myself, but everyone looked at me. I noticed Magnus staring at me; breaking whatever conversation he was carrying on with Amy. I think they all heard me. Magnus seemed to be looking at me, trying to figure something out.

I felt a tug on my shoulder. "Boss, you have to call the break. Everyone is waiting," Jessica said.

I paused to think for a second, confused by the entire situation. "You do it," I ended up saying. I couldn't leave this table—not now. She glared at me then stormed up to the stage.

Amy interjected, "Does anyone want a coffee?" Sarah and Magnus nodded. Jessica called the break over the mic.

"Tea, please," I said. I tried to ignore Magnus and concentrated again on Sarah. I could feel his eyes burning my profile, though. It was driving me crazy. I was finally face to face with the most beautiful creature on Earth and I couldn't say anything else. I could have called off the rest of the night to be alone with her. The place was packed; no private table we could go to.

"How long have you been here?" Sarah asked. I was lucky that she had broken the silence first.

Her question caught me off guard for some reason. I shook my head quickly. "Oh, quite some…" I caught myself, "…a few months or so. I don't really remember too much. It all seems to blur together. It's not the most exciting life."

"Well, that makes two of us," she said.

"I'm sorry, two of us?"

"With unexciting lives," she grimaced.

"I am sure your life gets pretty exciting," I replied.

"What makes you think that?" she asked.

"You probably get asked out on dates all the time. Beautiful women seem to have no problems getting jobs in today's society," I smiled as I spoke. "You look like you have a lot of exciting things going on in your life."

"I don't know. I guess I get out enough. I like going to concerts. I like the structured chaos of the music and dancing at them."

"Dancing?"

"Well, moshing. You know, slamming each other around. Oh, and I love crowd surfing." She seemed to really enjoy talking about these things.

"I've never been. But it sounds like fun," I paused. "Structured chaos, that is." I thought about these words more than anything else she was saying.

"Yeah, it is."

"Those words remind me of one of my old jobs," I added. "I kind of miss my old job."

"Oh yeah, what did you used to…"

I interrupted her, "What do you do? Oh, sorry, I didn't mean to interrupt." I did mean to interrupt her, though. I wasn't ready to answer her question. I had probably said too much already. I could feel Magnus staring at me. I tried to ignore him. I was growing uncomfortable with him sitting so close by.

"Oh, that's okay. I just got fired. Nothing fancy, I worked in the mall. I'm trying to go to college and all, but not really sure what I want to major in. I was thinking psychology or political science." Sarah stopped her answer as Amy came back with our drinks.

Amy looked at Magnus with a seductive smile and said, "Black and hot," as she handed him the coffee, diverting his attention from me. We all thanked her. She continued, "What are we talking about?"

"You know, the normal 'what do you do' beginnings of getting to know someone," Sarah replied. Her "matter-of-fact" way of talking was alluring. I had always tried to be direct like her, but I had some things to hide. She smiled at me.

Amy took her seat. Her and Magnus began to talk to one another in their own private conversation. I was finally able to ignore him. I took a quick look around the café and noticed that everyone was back in his or her seats. A few of the patrons looked a bit restless. We were so busy talking that I did not realize that the break was running long.

"I'm sorry, Sarah, I have to keep this thing going. Maybe we can do something afterward," I said, thinking it would be a good way to ask her out.

"That would be nice," she replied.

Of course, I hadn't thought of what that something would be, but

I felt it would really be *something*. I couldn't believe it was that easy. I made my way to the front of the café and grabbed the microphone. "I hope everyone is enjoying the night and the beverages. Let's continue this thing with a poem from Scott." A tall man with a Mohawk haircut and a goatee walked to the front. He seemed to me to be quite a menacing presence. He was dressed somewhat abnormally. He wore a pair of torn, dark brown cargo pants and a loose khaki sweater. His shoes looked expensive and he had a pinky ring with a large garnet in it, accented with diamonds. I handed him the mic and went back to the table.

Scott started talking. He had a soft voice. "This may well be my most favorite poem. Well, at least of the ones I have written. I won't deny that it is the exact description of who I am, but I would also like to point out that it seems so many people will deny the hypocrite inside of them. Of course, sometimes, these observances are through the eyes of the beholder, but it is good to step outside ourselves, from time to time, and take a look from a different perspective. This one is called 'Hypocrite':

I am the conservative punk
The moral anarchist
The angel that disbelieves
The godless Christ.

I am the militaristic pacifier
The gentle beast
War is the answer
But not with the fist.

I am the shy out-goer
The aggressively calm
Answer any question

But never sing the psalm.

I am the giving capitalist
The big-tip pauper
Will give away my possession
But always the shopper.

I am the oxymoron
The serious fool
An opaque chameleon
Hypocrisy's my tool."

I didn't think too much about Scott's poem as I made my way back up to the microphone. Everyone in the café, though, seemed to really be thinking about his words. I just wanted to get this open mic night over as fast as possible so I could be alone with Sarah. The bigger problem was, I only had a little bit of time to think of something to do with her.

"Thank you, Scott. I really enjoyed that," I said as merely a courtesy. "Next is Cassie. Cassie?" A contingent of girls screamed loudly from one of the tables as I said the name. "Looks like you brought your fan club. Come on up, you're next."

A somewhat plump girl walked up to the microphone. She wore a dark blue sweatshirt with college lettering on it. Her girlfriends cheered loudly as she hopped up on stage and put her hands in the air. "How is everyone doing tonight?" she asked as she grabbed the microphone away from me. I went back to the table to get out of her way quickly. She continued, "This is a poem that I wrote a couple months back, its titled Rebirth:

The golden rain poured from above.
It was the beautiful joy of love.

So many things in my past...
But I've finally had my last.
Memories cannot be thrown away.
You grow with them, with every day.
I am glad I have had mine,
But I need no more to find.
I have finally changed my life,
And pulled away from the strife.
I looked into the spring mist...
And felt the growing heartbeat in my wrist."

The patrons applauded and an ear-to-ear smile appeared on Cassie's face. "Thank you all *so* much," she acknowledged the crowd. Her friends were really going overboard with their applause.

I got to the front as quickly as possible. "Excellent poem, Cassie. We all enjoyed that very much," I said, purposely boosting her ego. I did enjoy the poem, but I was in a hurry. "Thank you."

She didn't seem to want to get off of the stage. I may have been mistaken, but I thought I saw a tear in her eye. I needed to keep this thing going and get these people out. "Cassie..." I was going to say her last name but forgot it, "ladies and gentlemen."

She noticed me searching for it, though. "Cassie Stevens," she added as she leaned into the mic.

"Cassie Stevens." I bent down to try and make it obvious to her that I was looking at the list. She barely budged. I put my hand on her shoulder and then open-handedly pointed to her seat. "Thank you, Cassie," I said once more. "Next up is Bryan Sayers. It looks like he will be playing a song for us. Bryan?"

Bryan had on a white button-down shirt with the top two buttons undone and collar upturned. Around his neck was a beaded hemp rope. His shirt was tucked into a pair of factory-torn jeans. He carried a guitar as he walked up to the front. Giving him the mic, I headed back to the table, again.

"This one is called 'Tides.' I wrote this one-day when I was on vacation in the OBX. I hope you all enjoy it:

I thought I could cross the ocean
One step at a time
Walking on white-capped waves
So high and so sublime.

He sang the first verse of the song with just his voice, before coming in with his guitar...

"I thought I knew the ocean's ways
How it rose and fell
Etching out the tortured landscape
Its story yet to tell.

I thought I let the ocean be
Stepping back to shore
Yet it buries my feet in sand
Locking me at its door.

I thought I heard the ocean sing
A song of salt and brine
But it loves its purpose here on Earth
Mirror Moon and Sunshine.

I thought I turned the ocean's heart
Against me by mistake
It crept up and melted my castles
Leaving me in its wake.

I thought I would give the ocean
A hand for awhile
And help to tell its great story
Together with a smile.

I thought I should wait for the ocean
To somehow forgive me
Before staring paralyzed at its power
And worldly beauty.

I thought I walked the ocean's edge
To gain new insight
To the life it gives us all here
In darkness and in light.

I thought I loved the ocean's breeze
The smell and its might
I thought I felt forever wrong
In feeling something right.

I thought I caught the ocean speak
As I turned to walk away,
"You may never know all that I am
But thank you for today."

I thought I dreamed that the ocean
Whispered in my ear,
"We may live through our tides apart
But as one we'll persevere."

I thought I smiled when the ocean smiled
"Friends 'til the end,"

Then I knelt down at the ocean's feet
And kissed the ocean's hand."

I stared at Sarah throughout the entire song. She was really into the song. I'm not sure if she knew I was looking at her. The moment seemed perfect. A melodic song filling my ears, a beautiful lady in my eyes, her wonderful scent in my nose, and…I slowly reached my hand to hers…

"Boss, the song is over," Jessica interrupted.

Sarah's hand grazed the top of mine just before I jumped up from the table in response to Jessica. Like a soldier snapping to his commander's every word, I instinctively marched up front.

"That was a great song, Bryan. Thank you." I think that was the loudest the applause had been all evening, not counting Cassie Stevens's fan club. I waited a few seconds for the noise to die down a bit. "Um…the next on the list is Mike Weaver." I waited to see someone make a motion. Nothing. "Well, it looks like Mike is gone."

"Hold up," a kid said, walking from the hallway that led to the bathrooms.

"You're up, Mike. After him will be the last poem of the night, which will be by…" I looked at the last name on the list. "…Magnus." I looked back at the table where Magnus, Amy, and Sarah were sitting. Amy and Sarah looked at Magnus and smiled. He didn't show any sign of emotion or concern.

Mike walked up the stage quietly with his head down. He had raggedy brown hair and wore a zipped-up sweatshirt. He got up on stage and raised his head, but not his eyes. I handed him the mic and went back to the table.

"This is my poem, called 'Treasure':

The blood of a young man's soul.
The luck of an honest dice roll.

The hatred of a muttered curse.
The lives stolen for a coin purse.
The men he has disposed.
The evil plans he has proposed.
The shame of this man's pride.
The crimes for which he died.
And what is their common seed?
This man's desire to need."

As I got up from the table, I glanced over to Magnus and gave him a nod to remind him that he was next. I made my way up to the microphone, passing Mike who looked as if he were running to the bathroom. Mike had left the mic on the stool. I picked it up. "Mike Weaver." I let the applause die down and continued, "You have to respect that kind of honesty. I know I do." I paused for a moment. "Last up is Magnus. But first, I hope you have all enjoyed this evening. You can count on more of these evening to come. Magnus?" I called his name again as he had yet to move from his seat.

Magnus looked up at me from his seat. He looked as if he wanted to make me feel uncomfortable by having me standing, holding the mic in my hand, waiting for him. I couldn't tell if he was smiling or smirking at me. He rose from the table in a manner that represented some imposed dominance over me—or so I imagined. He made his way methodically to the front. When he got to the front he stared at me. I offered him the microphone. He didn't take it. I offered it again. Again he didn't take it. Frustrated, I put the mic back on the stand and walked off the stage. I went back and sat with Sarah and Amy. Jessica joined us at the table.

Magnus took the microphone from the stand.

"The Fire

An open flame brings warmth to my soul,

69

And briefly reminds me of all that you stole.
The fire here has freedom with sadness.
The fire there has purpose with madness.
I stayed here knowing the danger of my choice.
I stayed there listening to the venom of your voice.
They sit here and waste away like ash.
You sit there and teach with a lash.
You must wonder why I choose to stay.
While I learn to savor every moment away.
Time seems to change for a seldom few
And not a one knows what is true.
We sit in the shadows knowing the evil is near.
While they live in joy without a care.
Envy I was. Envy I had become. Envy I remain.
I wish to have their hopes, their dreams, their pain.
But I stay in the shadows and watch from afar.
Knowing, full well, I will never be what they are.
For they are free of knowing what I know
Of the raging fire, burning far, down below."

I choked on my tea and spilled a bit down my chin. In an instant, everyone in the room seemed to disappear as Magnus walked off the stage. All around me the banana leaves showed signs of their fiery life, again. The night had changed. Magnus looked somewhat shook up after reading the poem and slowly walked toward the front door. Amy got up from the table and ran after him.

I glared at him as he walked out the front door and said to myself, "Now, this is interesting."

Chapter 7
Magnus and Samuel

"Coffee, black and hot."

"Good morning, Magnus," the clerk behind the counter retorted as he turned to face me. It was the manager of the coffee shop, Samuel. I looked into his dark, brown eyes and immediately knew that he recognized me. He did not just recognize me from last night. He remembered me from years before. It was the moment I hoped would never come. He must have figured it all out last night. He most likely spent the entire night pondering who I was and where he had met me before. If I had been smart, I would have been doing the same thing.

"Hello, Samuel. How are you?" I asked trying to act as if we were first acquainted last night.

"Not too well." He paused for a moment. "I know who you are."

"Come again?" I asked. I noticed no one else was in the coffee house. Usually another employee was present in the morning. But for some reason, it was only Samuel.

"I know who...what you are," he whispered to me.

"What is this nonsense you speak of?" I questioned as I looked toward the door. It was not far. I could probably make it. I could run away and be safe for another day.

"I served under you for a long time," Sam calmly said as he walked out from behind the counter and blocked my route to the door. He must have seen me glance at the door and wanted to make sure that I did not think of running. "I knew you by a different name back then. Funny, those seem to change when someone is looking for you."

I looked deep into his eyes to try and get a read on him. It was then that I finally recognized him. I could not remember his name, but I remembered his eyes. Many years ago he served under me. He was there when I left on my mission. It made sense that he was one of the many looking for me. He was a watcher, with an eye for detail. It would be him, or one like him, that would have the best chance of finding me.

"Why have you come?" I asked.

"Have a seat," he said pointing to a booth. "I'll get you your coffee and we'll talk."

I walked over to the booth and sat down as Sam went back behind the counter and poured the coffee. His back was to me. Now would be the best time to run. *What would be the use in trying?* He knew I was in the area. Others like him were surely around. All of them would be looking for me, their "Great Deserter". I always knew the day would come when they would find me. It was time to face my brethren, and my past, as a man.

He returned from behind the counter carrying a coffee. He put the coffee on the table in front of me. He walked to the front door and locked the bolt. He walked back to where I was at and sat facing me on the other side of the booth.

"What is your name?" I asked.

He stared at me blankly before replying, "Does it matter? You can keep calling me Sam if you like."

"I'm not who you think I am…" I started, hoping to lie my way out of the situation. He had to have been able to tell by my fast, strained speech that I was worried.

"Yes, you are," he replied calmly with a quaint smirk on his face.

It must have been a great relief for him to have finally caught me. I sat quietly and waited for him to make the next move. He did nothing. He sat and stared at me. He stared as if he had just finished a long journey, and was reflecting on the accomplishment. The chase was finally over, and he was finally content. He stared at me for nearly ten minutes before he said another word.

"Do you know how long I have been looking for you?"

"No," I replied.

"Since your betrayal and desertion."

My eyes widened in awe. I never thought they would send anyone for that long to look for me. He looked back at me and saw my reaction. He definitely knew that I was the one he was looking for.

"It does not have to end like this," I told him.

"Yes it does. It most certainly does. I have waited a long time in this land of confusion and waste. I have waited long, knowing that someday I would find you. They sent me to get you. Do you even realize how pissed off they are?"

"To hell with them! I am not their slave. I do not do what they tell me..."

"Yes, you do. We all do what they tell us to do, and they do what *he* tells them to do. It is the way we exist. It is what we are."

"Not anymore. I live here. I belong here."

"Here? You belong here?" he questioned me sarcastically. "Do you even know what you're saying? This place makes no sense. The people here drink and smoke, and cheat on their wives, and work in dead-end jobs, eat too much, cry too much, and feel sorry for themselves way too much. They live without rules. They live without true order."

"They live the way they want to live. They have that right. Do you think we would ever be allowed these rights where we come from?"

"We do not need rights, Magnus. We only need order. We exist knowing our purpose. We exist for our purpose. We are part of a system where authority and direction is all that matters. We know what our job is, and we do it. No questions asked, no thought of failure."

"And do you not find that sad?"

"What, that my service is with purpose? Of course not."

"But you do what they tell you to do, not because you want to do it, but because you have to. At the end of your time, you will have nothing to show for your service."

"Of course I will. I will have done my job."

"But to what end? You have no idea what deed came of your service, or if your service was even needed at all. All you will have, is what you made for yourself, which will be nothing."

He stared at me for a long time again before continuing. He was obviously contemplating his next course of action before pursuing.

"If you are trying to convince me that what you did is right, it will not work."

"What I did," I replied, "to your superiors, may seem wrong. But if you think about the situation, and everyone involved, I did the right thing."

"We do not decide what is right. You were given an order and you did not obey it. You are at fault. Just as I have been given an order to bring you back."

"The order I was given would have meant the lives of millions of men and women..."

"Forget them! They don't care about their lives anyway. You see it all the time here. Murderers, rapists, thieves. Then they meet us on the other side and beg for forgiveness. They should have been begging for it here! They are fools. Nothing more than animals, a herd of cattle, a flock without..."

"No! You are wrong. They are free. It is something we do not understand. They find joy in not knowing what tomorrow brings.

They enjoy the thrill of nearly dying. They like not knowing the grand scheme of things, of not having order, of not having to answer for every action they do. They live for the moment, for their friends, for their passions. They live to love and…"

"Finally we are seeing the point," Samuel laughed out loud as he clapped his hands together. "You want to be one of them. You want to spend the rest of your existence here, as one of them?"

I frowned and offered up an excuse, "No…I don't know."

"Ha. I never thought I would enjoy laughing, but I am. You make me laugh."

I sat quiet for a moment and allowed him to gloat before I continued. "So, you admit that you do enjoy things here?"

He stopped laughing immediately. I could tell he did not like that I was flipping the conversation to my favor.

"No. Not at all," Sam retorted.

"You know, you could never laugh like that before. If they ever saw you laughing like that, they would have you punished."

"That doesn't matter. I would gladly give up the right of laughter to have some order and reason. Do you not feel the same way?"

"I am afraid not."

"You are 'afraid not'? You speak of being afraid. We do not fear anything. Do you not remember what you did, and what you were? You were perfect. You did everything they wanted. No questions, no thoughts, and certainly no fears."

"I was a fool then."

"And now you're not?" Sam asked mockingly.

"No, now I see clearly. I see the error of my…our ways," I replied.

"Now all of those years of planning are forever lost. Does it not bother you that another must begin anew what you failed to finish?"

"Then let another begin anew," I told him defiantly.

"We can only hope he would be as meticulous as you."

"I am sure you will find one that is more than willing. It is not like I did anything that another could not do."

"Do you not remember what you did? No other could be so manipulative," Sam said proudly.

"I am sure another…"

"You started the first war by killing the Archduke…"

"You do not have to remind me…"

"You started the second by breeding that bastard from when he was born…"

"I know what I did…"

"All you had to do was start the third war…"

"I know what I did and did not do!" I yelled as I slammed my fist on the table. The cheap wood began to splinter along the tabletop.

Sam jumped back slightly from my reaction. "You should have finished your task," he added quietly.

"What was done was done. And I did the right thing."

"The right thing? You ran to the president of the United States. You told him everything. You told him that no missiles were on those boats, you told him it was all a farce and that you instigated the entire thing, and then you told him what we are and where we come from! You told him. A Catholic. Of all the people to tell, you tell a Catholic. You know how hard it was to eliminate him afterward? It was like the Almighty was watching over him."

"Apparently it was not that hard. He was dead not too long after."

"But then we had to eliminate his assassin to make sure no one followed the footsteps that led back to us."

"I am sorry," I said sarcastically, "I should have just let millions of people die. Because, I alone, should hold that power. I, alone, reserve the right to kill millions of humans because I was given an order.

"I had seen too much death already," I said changing my tone from sarcasm to sorrow. "I had been the cause of too many lost lives. It was time to walk away."

I could tell by his eyes that he was beginning to understand. He had dark brown eyes, almost lifeless eyes. I got a read on him. The one power I had over others was the ability to read their eyes. It was why I was chosen for the job all those years ago. I could look into their eyes and see their intentions, emotions, hopes, dreams, desires, failures, and remorse. When I could read their eyes, nothing was hidden from me. I looked into Sam's eyes, and saw a determined, but rational being.

"You do know," I pressed on, "That you will be punished when we return. I may have deserted them, but you have taken far too long to return. They are going to wonder what you were doing. And what are you to tell them? That you have been working in a coffee shop when you should have been looking for me? Do you think they will understand that? Do they understand anything? No jury where we come from. Only judgment. You will be found guilty."

"I must carry out my order."

"No, you do not have to. You have been sitting in this café discussing this with me. They would never approve of this. Nor would they approve of you having your own rational thoughts. Face it Samuel, you have already been assimilated into this society. It is not as bad as you think. All you have to do…is accept it."

He stopped talking and quietly stared at the table. He had to know as well as I did that the newfound taste for freedom would be missed if we should return home. Our brethren never allowed personal satisfaction or personal thought. They cared nothing for me, and surely cared nothing for him. I was a name in the hierarchy. Not much more than a name, but a name nonetheless. He was nothing. He was a lackey sent to bring a criminal back for persecution.

"How did you stay hidden for so long?" Sam asked as he lifted his eyes to meet my gaze. This was the question that I hoped he would ask. I knew that he was contemplating how he could stay.

"I did not worry about being found. I just created a life for myself, and went forward. Everyday I tried to be more like them. And until last night, I never came close."

"What about last night?"

"Everything: The atmosphere, the poetry, the coffee, the aroma, the carefree attitude, the woman. Everything was like a dream. Have you begun to dream yet Sam? That is when you know you belong."

Sam closed his eyes and clenched his fists. He began to talk, as if he was pulling his thoughts from memory, or reading them from a card. "My dreams are haunted with uneasiness. Alone in a sea of chaos, I fly. Like a god, I float over the entire Earth, or at least my world, and observe every aspect of life. I have no power to manipulate the surroundings. I have no power to help the struggling. I have no power to interact. No beautiful women in my dreams…no pain, either. I dream, with only the power to see it all. I have always seen all the angles. I have seen all of the sides to all of the stories…except my own."

"Now that sounds quite sad."

He opened his eyes and continued. Still talking as if he was reading from a card. "The only recognizable part of my dreams, are the fires. I guess staring at burning green images all day long while awake, translates into red flames in my dreams. The flames shoot up all around me, like red banana leaves and autumn forests. I travel over the highways and metropolitan cities. I see all of the injustices that are occurring every day in every way. I look upon desolation and realize that each human life is quite insignificant. I try to remember why I am even here. I have always felt that I am here from some greater purpose."

"It does not sound like a pleasant dream. At least not one that I would care to dream."

"What do you dream of, Magnus?"

"I dream of being like them. I dream of waking up in the morning next to someone who is happy to be by my side. I dream of shaking someone's hand and knowing that I can trust him. I dream of watching the sunset break upon the ocean as I watch the purple sky darken to meet the deep blue water. I dream of holding a child in my arms and not have it cry. I dream of meeting God and for Him to open His arms and tell me that all is forgiven."

"Those are things I do not think I could ever dream."

"You can…and you will."

"I cannot imagine how God can ever forgive the ones like us. How can I ever dream of it?"

"I could never imagine forgiveness either. For years I thought I would have to live alone with my sins forever. I think Amy changed all that for me. Being around her is indescribable. She bestows in me a purpose, a faith, and a trust that I never knew existed."

"Lately, I have become more aware of trust."

"How is that, Sam?"

"I seem to trust my employees and the people I know more everyday. I seem to trust Jessica, Amy, and especially Sarah. I seem to trust my emotions when I am around them."

"Those emotions will change, Sam. You will feel a freedom through those emotions that you would never have believed possible. When the emotions come, your freedom comes, and with it, your dreams will change. They will change as you change. You will dream of places and things that you and I were never meant to see."

"Well, my dreams have already changed as of late."

"What has changed?"

"My dreams now are less focused. I wake knowing I dreamt, but I don't remember what it is that I dreamed of. I do know the flames were near."

"I think the flames will always be near, Sam. They are in my dreams, too."

"I know."

"Excuse me?" I asked.

"Your poem last night. It's what gave you away."

I looked back at him and smiled. For the first time ever, I felt companionship. I thought Amy would be the only person who would ask me what my dreams and fears were. She would ask, but she would never understand. I knew only the ones from where I came from would ever truly understand. They would understand, but none of them would ever listen. For the first time ever, I was able to communicate my dreams to someone, and that someone, in return communicated his dreams to me. We not only listened to each other, we also understood each other. Not another soul in the world besides Sam and myself would ever understand.

As I lost myself further in my pondering, Sam spoke again: "Last night when the guy was reading the sonnet, I saw the flames. During which the banana leaf wallpaper burned around Sarah's beauty as I stared at her. It burned the image into my mind. It was the only time I ever felt like I was in the right place. I was surrounded by the marvel of social interaction, and I liked it. I could feel. The words that came through the speaker that night touched me. Touched me as I looked at Sarah and was awed by her beauty."

We sat quietly for quite some time. Customers came to the door and knocked to get in. Sam and I ignored them. They stared through the window at us, waiting for one of us to unlock the door, but we never did. We sat in each other's company both knowing that times had changed. We were free. We were free, and we were no longer alone. He had Sarah, and I had Amy. He had me, and I had him. In a matter of days I went from being alone in the world to having a woman that I cared about, and a friend who understood me. Everything was perfect.

"I should be going to work," I said breaking the silence.

Sam looked up at me as I got up from the booth. "I should probably open the café back up," he said, standing up from the booth.

"Probably a good idea, you do not want the customers calling the owner."

"No, that wouldn't be the best thing."

"My employees are probably wondering where I am at."

"Go to work Magnus. But don't go far. I have to make my decision."

"I think you already made it," I said sticking out my hand.

Sam smiled at me, and shook my hand, reassuring me that I was right. He had no intention of turning me in. He seemed to realize that what he had now was better than what he ever had before. He just needed time to sort it all out.

I unlocked the front door and stepped out onto the sidewalk. The sun was rising quickly and the glare from the parking lot was blinding. I looked back at Sam through the window and smiled at him. I had never trusted anyone before, but I trusted him not to turn me in. He had never trusted anyone before, but he trusted me not to run. We put our trust in a handshake.

I turned from the window and walked across the parking lot. My dreams were becoming reality.

Chapter 8
Aganes

.

I watched Magnus walk out the door. He looked back and smiled at me through the window, but I didn't return the gesture. I think he trusted me. I was unsure whether or not that trust was misplaced. He seemed confident that I would not turn him in, confident that I would disobey my order. I felt a sinking sensation in my stomach.

I rushed to the bathroom and slammed down onto my knees in front of the toilet bowl. I stared down into the water in the bowl with my mouth open wide. My stomach wrenched and I dry-coughed a few times. My throat swelled up and was really sore. The water in the bowl rippled slightly from my breath. I looked down at my reflection in the water. My face looked extremely pale. After about the fifth dry heave, tears rolled down my face and dripped slowly into the toilet. I slumped backward, resting against the back wall.

I heard pounding coming from the back door. I grabbed a hold of the handicap bar and propped myself up. The pounding continued. I took a look in the mirror. My face was still pale. I splashed some water on my face, dried off, and went to the back room. I opened the back door. Jessica stood outside.

"Good morning, boss! Sorry I'm late. I have no excuse," Jessica greeted me as she walked into the back room. She took off her jacket and hung it on one of the coat hooks. She put on her apron as she walked to the front of the store. I slowly followed behind her. "I tried knocking on the front door, but no one answered. I saw your car though, so I figured you were in the backroom," she said. She turned around as she pushed open the saloon doors and looked back at me. "You don't look so well."

"Can you take over by yourself? I really need to go home." I got straight to the point. "I will call someone else in to help you."

"Sure…what's wrong, boss?" Jessica asked with a concerned look.

"I just have to go home. My stomach isn't going to let me be too productive today. Thanks, Jessica." I said as I struggled to smile through my mental anguish.

The ride home in the morning light was agonizing. The sun burned my eyes, as I had to drive toward it to get home. My eyes diverted from the road to stare at myself in the rearview mirror. Bloodshot from crying and inner turmoil, the whites of my eyes looked like they were on fire. Despite my incoherent driving, I made it home.

I had a lot to ponder. I was anxious, but scared for some reason. Scared of what I might decide. Scared that maybe, ultimately, it wasn't my decision, anyway. Deep down I felt what I imagined to be hope. Hope, I didn't quite understand. My head was pounding. The hope was mixed with terror. I was terrified of all the things that could happen since I found out who Magnus really was. But, hope remained. All of the scenarios played out in my head. The tea wasn't cutting it. I made a cup of instant coffee. That is all I had at my apartment. The day and night were restless.

I'm not sure if I got any sleep that night. If I did, I surely didn't remember any dreams I may have had. If only I could have dreamt and seen the fires again. After my discussion with Magnus, this world had changed for me. Actually, both worlds had changed for me. It was ironic, the one I was sent to find all those years ago, was working next door to where I worked. Things were different, though. I felt what I could only equate to what is considered humanity. I felt the things that Magnus told me. I felt them and understood them—desired them. Beyond all that, however, two words loomed over my sleepless night—duty and consequence.

I got ready for work. I had to go back to the café. I had to face up to my duties, to deal with the consequences of finding Magnus, to confront those that would judge me for who I was or what I was going to do—whether I knew the outcome or not. I was still unsure of what I was going to do. Everything I had known here could be gone in an instant if I wasn't careful. I could lose the only friendship—or link to humanity—I had ever had in my entire existence. I could lose Sarah. *Was I ready to accept the consequence of my actions?*

On my way to work, the trees were trees for once—no fires. The world looked different. The café looked different. When I turned on the lights and the music in the store, the banana leaves didn't catch fire. I could feel the rhythmic tunes pulsating my eardrums. The music was enchanting. I went to the front window. I stood still and stared outside. I watched the few cars on the street pass by. Cars were generally few and far between early on a Saturday morning. I knew we would be busy, though.

I stopped staring out of the front window when a car pulled into the lot. It was Jessica arriving to work. She looked beautiful in her work clothes as she got out of her car. Her hair, like a flag in the wind, swayed majestically in the breeze. I wasn't attracted to her as Jessica, but as an embodiment of the female form.

She walked through the door and smiled at me. "Good morning, boss," she said.

"Good morning, Jessica," I replied. It felt like it was the first time I had ever used such pleasantries. I smiled back at her. I think I saw her turn a bit red as she passed.

I made a pot of coffee. I knew how to make the perfect pot of coffee according to the guidelines that I had learned, but I had never tasted that which I made. I had always taken the customer's word for it. It took the proper amount of coffee and good water to make the coffee just right. I got excited waiting for the pot to brew. I stood close by in order to inhale the aroma. The café always smelled like coffee, but I had never let myself become so consumed by its essence. The last drops of coffee-infused water dripped into the serving decanter.

I poured myself a cup and took a sip. The taste was exquisite. The instant coffee I drank the previous night wasn't very good. This coffee, however, slapped my taste buds alive. The earthen taste was more powerful than any tea could ever become. The bitter acid of the coffee soothed my scratchy throat. I felt the coffee's power fill my head.

"What are you doing? You don't drink coffee."

I just smiled at her.

We went through the morning rituals necessary to get the shop opened. We worked with a comfortable silence between us. We enjoyed the jazzy morning music as we prepared the coffee and pastries. The time went by quickly. A customer was standing outside ready for his morning coffee. I opened the front door and let him in. I served him his morning coffee with a smile. He left with a smile.

"What's with you?" Jessica asked.

"What? I am not allowed to smile?" I jeered.

"Yeah, but I have never seen you smile like that. Did you and Sarah get it on or something?"

"What?" I exclaimed as I shot her a look, letting her know that I found her comment inappropriate.

"Well, you two were hitting it off the other night and you took yesterday off. We all just figured…" Jessica stopped.

"We?" I gave her the same look as before. "Am I the subject for today's gossip?" I wasn't angry, but more intrigued at the notion that people were discussing *my* personal life. This was definitely something new to me. They had probably talked about me in the past; I wasn't naïve. However, it was the first time I was ever told about it.

"That's what you did yesterday, wasn't it?" Jessica kept prodding.

"Not that it's your business, but no. I was sick." I understood why she was questioning me, as I had never called in sick before.

"I think I remember you demanding the truth out of us all the time."

"I am telling the truth. Ask Sarah next time she comes in."

"Maybe I will," Jessica mocked.

"You don't trust me?" I mocked back.

Jessica didn't answer me. We got back to work finishing up the morning routine. All the different flavors of coffee were made and the pastries were baked and displayed. As we finished, Magnus walked in.

"Coffee, black and hot," Magnus said without expression. He tried to lock his eyes on mine.

I didn't look up at him. I knew he was waiting for me to look him in the eyes. He left the other day seeming confident in my trust. He had to be thinking of our origins, though. I knew he came in to find out for sure. I didn't think I could lie with my eyes, so I kept myself occupied with getting his coffee.

I handed him his coffee and he handed me his money. That was the only time he had not just laid his money on the counter. He actually handed it to me. He turned and left the café.

"What was that about, boss?"

"You don't want to know," I answered.

As the dawn subsided, I got swept up in the momentum of the morning activity. People coming and going, coffee practically flying around behind the counter, my employees running back and forth, and customers getting their morning fix; it all made me smile. On the weekends, people hung around for longer in the morning. They didn't have much else to do. At last, it all made sense to me. It felt good to see that maybe some order did exist here: an order to waking up everyday, getting that cup of coffee, and shuffling off to work. Then enjoying the peace and relaxation from winding down on the weekends. I began to understand the duty in nearly every mundane job that people had invented. Even if they weren't solving some major issue—which many were doing at home on a daily basis, I learned—they could find some tranquility in their day-to-day routines.

I started interacting with the customers more than I ever had in the past. I asked them about their jobs and lives. I asked them why they worked nine to five daily for a company that they hated or at a job they didn't enjoy. I wanted the answers to what it meant to feel "human."

Family was the reason that seemed to matter most. Most worked long, hard hours for their families. Most "suck it up and drive on" to provide their families with the best opportunities. They did it to see their kids grow up in the best neighborhoods and get the best educations. I never really had a family, nor much of a secular education. I went to colleges, but I was mostly an observer. I was a predator stalking my prey. My life was designed around duty. I lived under a hierarchy and I was just one of many who had to do the legwork when asked. I was a soldier in the most infernal army.

I tried to talk about my past to a few of the customers, but words to describe where I had come from were hard to find. To them, I must have looked sad. I had seen things they would only dream about in their worst nightmares. I couldn't say any of it with a smile anymore, but I didn't want to depress the customers either. What little I could get out about my past felt good, though.

As the morning rush began to die down, I contemplated what my next action would be with Magnus. I was still unsure of the choice I was going to make. I was in a unique position for the first time in my life. I had the upper hand over the ones I used to be subservient to. I wasn't the only one here looking for him. I was sure of that. The Earth is a big place and our kind's methods aren't "state-of-the-art." I guessed that about one hundred of us would be after him, at least.

Things were different since I found him, though. I had the power. I believed in what Magnus was saying the other day. I saw things here and believed in things here that I had never felt before. I felt like I was finally beginning to understand the concept of hope. I felt the connections that men and women feel. I knew, however, that if I did not turn Magnus in, I would be hunted down and would suffer the same fate as him. I was not as crafty as he was and would have never been able to hide for that long. *Maybe I could use him as a bargaining chip. Maybe I could convince them to let me stay here.* It was a long shot, but it was the newfound hope that was driving me.

I went into the back to my office space. I nervously reached into my back pocket and pulled out my cell phone. I stared at Aggie's number. My training as an infernal soldier took over any thoughts and inhibitions I may have acquired in my growth in humanity. I called Aggie. I was obligated to report. I couldn't stop myself.

The familiar voice answered, "This is Aggie."

"This is Samsapeel," I said softly.

"You've found him?" asked Aggie aggressively.

I gulped. "I…I am not sure, yet," I replied. "I think I am close. I just need a little bit more time."

"Then why are you using your real name?" Aggie asked, seeming slightly menacing.

"None of the others can possibly be this close," I responded more confidently.

"I am on my way."

I hesitated. "Wait. Don't come here yet," I said, trying not to sound too demanding. I knew he wouldn't appreciate me ordering him around, but I needed more time to figure this out.

"What did you just say to me?" his voice hissed.

"I have to go." I abruptly ended the conversation.

As I hung up the phone I barely made out the voice on the other end as it said, "I am coming to get you."

The conversation seemed like a dream. After it was over, I couldn't remember even picking the phone up or anything that Aggie said. *"What have I done?"* I thought out loud. *"I think I turned us in. How soon would he be here?"*

I picked up the café's phone and dialed the number for the grocery store next door.

Someone answered, "Thank you for calling..."

I hung up right away. I stared at the phone. I reached for it, again. Someone tapped me on the shoulder.

"Are you okay?" Jessica asked. I didn't hear her come into the office.

"What?" I answered, "Oh. Yes. Let's get back to work." I stood up and walked with Jessica to the saloon doors leading to the front counter.

"No customers and I have already cleaned up everything, boss," Jessica said.

I looked over the café and saw that she was right. "Well, why don't you take a break?" I turned around and headed back to the office space.

"Okay. I'll be studying..." her voice trailed off.

I sat back down at my desk and stared at the computer monitor. Looking at my reflection in the screen, I realized that I looked really sad—pathetic even. I picked up the phone again. I dialed the grocery store number. The same voice answered and I hung up on him again. I stood up quickly and went back out to the front of the store.

"Jessica?" I called to her as if to ask her a question.

"Yes, boss?" she replied, as she looked up from her book.

"I have to ask you something," I said as I walked over and sat across from her at the booth she was at.

She stared at me. Her eyes appeared to have a sparkle in them.

"Yes," she said.

"What do you consider is the best thing about being here?" I asked.

"You mean, here, at the café?"

"Yes, but no, I mean, here on Earth," I paused. "Not just that...why do we do this?" I didn't know where I was going with the questioning.

"I don't think I understand," she told me.

"All people seem to do things both selflessly and selfishly. Ultimately, though, they do what is necessary to survive within the parameters of the life they want for themselves. They claim that they do what they do because of their family or friends. But isn't it more about doing the things that are necessary to keep one happy? If that means making family and friends happy, then that is what one does. But one survives by taking care of oneself first." I started to confuse myself. I paused for a few seconds then continued, "I'm just trying to understand what makes us decide to do one thing over another."

Jessica replied, "I have always felt that we do what we feel is right."

"Then how do you live with each decision?" I asked.

"Is something wrong?" she asked back.

"Something I have done. I had a conversation with someone on the phone and I am not really sure why I did it. Something bad may happen. At any rate, I feel bad about something I did," I rambled. I got up and looked out the front window. The sky was beautiful.

"You have the opportunity to look at this sky every day. Yet, you choose to be sheltered and stay inside."

Jessica didn't say anything. I looked back at her and she was just staring at me. I caught her smile as I turned back to look out the window again.

As I was about to turn around I saw a car pull into the lot. It was a somewhat ordinary car, however, I immediately recognized the driver. He was older, his hair gray, close-cropped, and his blue eyes cut through me from twenty yards away. I watched him park in front of the café and get out of his car. He labored to get out of the car, using the door as a crutch. It was an obvious act. He never took his eyes off of me. A breeze caught his khaki trench coat as he slammed his car door closed. He reached up and put a speckled, gray hat onto his head. He walked toward the café and I opened the door for him.

"Hello, Aggie," I greeted him.

"Thank you. Today you will call me Aganes," he said firmly. "Lock the door behind me and send that person away." He pointed to Jessica.

Jessica had gone back to work cleaning and doing the final preparation for the lunch rush. She didn't seem to see Aganes point to her or tell me to send her away. I walked over to her as Aganes took a seat at one of the booths.

"Jessica?" I asked to get her attention.

She looked around the café before looking at me. "Who is that?" she nodded over to Aganes.

"He is an old friend of mine. Listen, I need you to take a break for a bit. But, I need you to leave the store," I said politely.

"Why?"

"Well, I need to talk some business with my friend and we need complete privacy. This is very important."

"What's going on? Who is he? Is everything okay?" she said nervously.

91

"Just please do this for me," I pleaded. If I couldn't get her out of the café politely, I knew Aganes would take matters into his own hands. "Please, Jessica."

She paused and stared at me for a few seconds, then said hesitantly, "O…Okay, boss. I'll be across the street. When should I be back?"

"Check back in about a half an hour. If that man is still here, then stay away. Okay?"

"Okay."

"Thank you, Jessica. Maybe I will be able to explain this to you someday," I added. I leaned over the counter and kissed Jessica on the cheek. It went against all of my instincts, but I did it.

Jessica turned the brightest shade of pink I had ever seen anyone turn. She looked at me for a second then rushed into the back room. She came back out with her coat and purse and smiled at me. We headed to the front door and I let her out, locking the door behind her. She turned around one last time to smile at me once more. She walked away and I was alone with Aganes.

I sat opposite Aganes at the booth. He had taken off his coat and hat. He had on a dark blue dress shirt and a solid red tie. He stared at me with his blue eyes. I wondered if he could see the sadness in my eyes.

"Do you have something you want to tell me?" he asked graciously.

I was unsure of where to start. I wanted to figure out what he knew about these emotions I was feeling, the fires, the purpose of our search, and our time here. I was hoping he could help me with these questions. However, I knew that wasn't why he was here. He wanted to know where Haborym was. I knew, that he knew, that I knew where Haborym was. *How long could I conceal that knowledge from him? Would he make me crack? Would I succumb to order and duty, and give away Magnus's location?*

"You needn't suppress your thoughts around me, Samsapeel. I know what you desire. I know that you see the fires. I know that you long to be with these women. We have all, at some point, gone through those phases," he said, using a mentor's voice. "We, however, are here to do a duty."

"Where does that leave us, though?" I questioned defiantly.

"You dare ask such a question?" His voice was both angry and disappointed.

"What purpose does our duty serve?"

"I am afraid you have been here too long. Only the strongest amongst our kind can survive here for a long time. You are weak." His disappointment was apparent in his voice and body language. He diverted his gaze from mine and continued, "I can no longer look at you."

Aganes was the one person I had never wanted to disappoint. My eyes began to tear. I wiped my eyes before the tears could run down my face.

Aganes noticed my gesture and goaded, "Look at you. What is wrong with you? You were one of my most favored pupils. Now, you are nothing more than a lost soul."

My tears kept flowing; however, they were slowly changing from tears of sadness to tears of anger.

He kept mocking me. "Pull yourself together. Haven't you learned, through your time here, that you can never be like them? They will never understand you, and you will never understand them. Haven't you listened to me all these years? The fires will never stop, Samsapeel. It is your need to be back home. Nothing will ever change that. You are what you are. And from the looks of it, you are nothing more than a pathetic has-been who has lost his way."

I was at the height of my fury. "A pathetic has-been who has found Haborym!" I stood up and stormed away from Aganes. I went to the front door, unlocked it, and went outside. I saw Jessica sitting in her car. She was staring back at me. She motioned as if she were getting out of the car and I signaled for her to stay where she was. She rolled her eyes at me in protest, but stayed in the car. I smiled back at her. She pointed at something over my shoulder.

I hadn't noticed that Aganes had followed me out, until he grabbed my shoulder from behind. I saw Jessica grimace.

"Where?" he growled, as he squeezed my shoulder and dug his fingers into my muscle.

I was much bigger and stronger than him, but I had no desire to fight him. He had the power to bring a lifetime of wrath upon me. I answered, "I want to stay here." I turned my gaze from Jessica and stared up at the sun.

"What did you say?"

I kept looking at the sun while he dug his fingers further into my shoulder muscle. "I said, I want to stay here," I said more calmly, but louder.

"Stay? Here? You would grow crazier than you already are. Trust me," he said as he loosened his grip. "Do you even know what 'here' is? Do you even know what that word means to us? You say things like 'here' and 'there,' but have forgotten what they mean. We do not belong 'here'. We belong 'there.'"

"Nevertheless, I want to stay. I'll tell you where Haborym is at, in exchange you allow me to remain here." I tried to be assertive.

"We do not get rewards. Nor do we ask for them," he replied.

"God rewards those that serve Him," I came back with.

"Where did you hear that nonsense?" he paused. "Anyhow, you do not work for Him. You work for us. And we do things a little differently."

"I want to stay," I said again, fully assertive. "I'll tell you where he is, if you let me stay here."

"I am not sure I can trust you anymore. Not after that display you just showed me. You are too weak and ignorant to have found someone as powerful as Haborym."

"Do we have a deal?" I wasn't going to let him goad me again. He spun me around and stared me in the eyes. I saw my reflection in his glassy, blue eyes. The sun also reflected within his gaze, making my image look like it was on fire. I smiled as I stared at myself engulfed in flames through his eyes.

"Do we have a deal?" I repeated.

"If you are not lying to me…" he began.

I interrupted, "I am not lying to you."

He didn't acknowledge my words and finished, "…then we have a deal."

"Good."

"If you are lying to me…"

Slightly angered, I interrupted again, "I am not lying to you."

He again finished without acknowledging my words, "…then we have a problem."

"For the last time," I shouted, "I am not lying to you!"

"I will hunt you down and destroy you." He stared right through me.

I settled down and asked calmly, "Do we have a deal?"

He nodded. I wanted to hear him say the words, though.

He continued, "You are making a big mistake. You will find out soon enough that I am right. You are going to hate it here without purpose, without duty. These women will betray you." He looked over my shoulder at Jessica. "They will betray your emotions, just like they did to us in the beginning. You better never forget where you come from and who you are. It is the only thing that will keep you sane."

"Then we have a deal?" I tried to ignore his words.

"We have a deal." He paused before continuing. "Where is he?"

I believed him. Somehow, even after everything that transpired, I still trusted him. Magnus was out in the parking lot gathering the grocery store's carts. I pointed to him. "That's him."

Chapter 9
Haborym

"Coffee, black and hot."

Sam said nothing as he grabbed a cup and made my coffee. He kept his head down and acted like I was not even in the café. I hoped that he would raise his head and look me in the eye. He never did. He made the coffee and handed it to me.

I took the money out of my pocket and put it in his hand as I took the cup of coffee from him. I saw for a brief moment that he had a slight look of shock. I had always put the money on the counter. Never before had I put it in his hand. He must have known this, too. He turned away and put the money in the register. I was alone at the counter. Alone again. I quickly turned and walked toward the exit.

I walked the sidewalk that led from the coffeehouse to the marketplace, with an empty feeling. I could not figure out why Sam acted the way he did. It seemed the day before that we had come to terms with our existences and we would be able to trust each other. Perhaps all of that had changed.

I unlocked the automatic doors at the entrance to the marketplace. A young man and woman got out of their cars and walked toward the front door. It was the morning stocker and cashier.

"Hi, Magnus," the woman said to me.

"What's new?" the young man asked me.

"Good morning," I replied.

They looked at each other as they walked in through the automatic doors. I did not think the employees would ever grow used to me using pleasantries. I was not sure if I would grow used to it either. I put my head down to avoid their stares as I walked into the store.

I let the employees do their work as I went into the office. Like every morning, I prepared the register drawers for the day's sales. I did it the same as I had any other morning, but for some reason I finally saw how important it was. Without preparing the drawers, no sales would be made for the day. Without the sales, none of the customers would buy the commodities they needed. If the customers did not get what they needed, they could not prepare food at their restaurants for the consumers. The entire importance of the job began to appear before me: Why I stocked the store, why the manager looked at sales numbers, why the cashiers complained, why the stockers screwed around. Everything made sense to me. I was a key piece of an overly inefficient machine. It was not a system that I was used to. But, it was a system with responsibility and duty, and most importantly, reward. I felt good that I made the store look good. I got a paycheck for doing so. Customers were happy when the product they wanted was on the shelf.

I looked at the clock and noticed we were about to open. I had been thinking about the situation longer than I thought. I walked out of the office and saw that the cashier was letting in a few customers. She was letting them in early. She said "hello" to them as they walked into the store. A smile came across my face. Perhaps the cashiers were not completely useless. I noticed the stocker helping one of the customers locate an item they were looking for. Perhaps the stockers did do some work. They did the little things as I did the big one: I stocked the store and made it look perfect.

I walked past a customer and nodded my head. "Hello."

"Sir, could you tell me where your boneless, skinless, chicken breasts are?" he asked me.

"They are in aisle seven. I can show you, if you would like to follow me?"

I handed the register drawer to the cashier. "You will probably need this."

She smiled at me. It was not like me to make such comments, and she knew it. The customer followed behind me as I walked to aisle seven. I pointed to the door that had the chicken breasts. "Top shelf is the skin-on. Bottom shelf is the skinless."

"Thank you."

"Anything else, sir?"

"No, thanks."

As I turned I saw another customer looking my way. She was an older lady with a brown sweater and brown slacks. She was trying to make eye contact with me to get my attention. Usually I would pretend like I did not see her looking at me and head the other way. Not this time. I walked up to her and offered my assistance.

"Anything I can help you with today, ma'am?

"Yes, why does this bag of shrimp cost more than this one?" she asked holding a bag of shrimp in each hand.

"Well, it depends on the size. Shrimp is packaged by count per pound. The bottom shelf is the U-fifteen, which means you will have at least fifteen shrimp per pound. Those are the biggest we carry. The next shelf is sixteen to twenty-four count, which means you will have twenty shrimp per pound on average. The next shelf is…"

"Oh, I see. That makes a lot sense. So these are thirty-one to forty-five count. They're cheaper because they're smaller."

"Exactly."

"Thank you, very much."

"Not a problem. Anything else I can help you with?"

"No. Thanks."

"Have a nice day," I finished with a smile.

My new outlook on the job, and these people, gave me fulfillment I never knew before. The interactions with the customers had me completely distracted from the incident in the morning with Sam. I knew he needed time to sort everything out. I would let him come to his own conclusion about what to do. I was quite confident that he knew that neither him nor I could ever return home. We had tasted freedom, and would never let go. The flames would always remind us, and call us home. But other comforts existed here that could take their place.

It seemed that my discussion with Sam brought forth more resolve in myself about staying here. It seemed that I was not only explaining why we should stay to Sam, but I was also explaining it to myself. I had been trying for years to fit in with the populace in every way. I never succeeded until this day. I finally felt that I was a part of something. I was part of the team that worked at the marketplace, which in turn, was part of the community. A series of systems built upon one another. Every system needed people to work within them, but not every person needed to work well for the system to survive. Redundant work. Unimportant work. Bad work. It did not matter. The system worked so long as everyone was working. Order with chaos. Give with reward. Freedom with responsibility. The balance fulfilled.

I walked back to the front of the store. The cashier turned to face me. She had a large smile on her face.

"What has gotten into you today?" she asked me, tilting her head slightly.

"I do not know," I answered, with a laughing smile.

"Did you have a good date or something?"

"Well, yes…I mean, no. Not last night. But, yes, I did have a good date recently."

"Crazy how those can change your outlook."

I wondered what she meant by that comment. *Could it be Amy that was causing this change in me? Could all of this be stemming from the emotions that she raised in me? Was I finally seeing the way to become what I wanted to be, because of a woman?*

"Maybe..." I said quietly.

The cashier was walking toward the front door.

"I'm gonna get carts," she said.

"I can get them. You can stay and watch the register."

"Thanks," she replied.

I smiled back at her as I walked out the front door. I had never gotten carts for the cashiers. I always thought it was the least they could do as they ate cookies and complained about the customers. But I did not feel that way anymore. I was happy to help her out. I wanted to do my part; I wanted to do more. I wanted to make the marketplace a good place to work.

I walked around the parking lot gathering the carts. Like always, they were sprawled out across the parking lot. Not a single one was in the cart corral that the marketplace provided. The customers had a way of leaving them pushed up on the lawn, or leaning on someone's car. It was rude, but it did not bother me. I took advantage of the time needed to gather the carts to enjoy the sun that was radiating its warmth down upon me.

I finished gathering the carts and had them lined up ready to go into the store. I looked across the parking lot at the coffeehouse. I wondered if Amy would be working later. It would be nice to go on another date with her. The warmth from the sun was comforting, but the memory of her kiss was even more so. The flames may call me home, but I knew they would never convince me.

As I looked at the coffeehouse, Sam came walking out the front door with another behind him. I tried to wave to him, but I do not think he saw me. He was probably busy with the guy he was talking to. It was probably a customer, or someone who is looking for directions. It was strange that the man appeared to have his hand on Sam's shoulder. I thought nothing else of it. I shrugged my shoulders. Maybe I would talk to Sam later about it. I pushed the carts toward the front door. They rattled along noisily, bumping up and down on the rough asphalt.

I pushed the carts in the door and guided them into their resting place along the wall. I turned around to see an old man in a khaki trench coat and a gray speckled hat standing at the door, about ten feet away from me. He seemed to have appeared out of nowhere. I quickly noticed it was the person Sam was talking to in the parking lot. *How did he get across the parking lot so fast?* He had a devilish smile on his face and his blue eyes pierced me with an unworldly stare.

He took a couple of steps toward me and spoke. "Hello, Haborym."

My heart sunk to my knees. My entire existence crashed down in front of me. They had found me. Sam had betrayed me. The lie was over. I stumbled backwards.

"You do not know how long I have waited for this," the old man said, stepping closer to me. He planted his feet sturdily and watched my reaction.

I regained some of my composure and stood up straight. "You were never one to hide your identity, were you Aganes?"

"I am glad you know who I am. I want all to know that it was I, Aganes, who captured the elusive, traitorous, Haborym."

I felt a rage of fire come through me. I had come too far in the past week to lose it all to him. I stepped forward and planted my feet in defiance. "You have not captured me yet."

"Please, do not make a fool of yourself. Your power is with persuasion, Haborym, not strength. You cannot fight me."

I knew he was right. I could not fight him…nor did I want to. My quick stance of defiance was a mere misapprehension for what I truly felt—betrayal. Sam had betrayed me, and it took him only a day to decide to do so. It was only a day ago that we sat at the coffeehouse and talked about all the reasons to stay. He had me completely fooled. I actually thought he would come around. I thought that he would stay. I thought that he had realized how good everything was here. I thought he was a friend. I thought I could trust our handshake.

Customers were still coming in and out of the store. I glanced around to them as they walked by. Most of them ignored us; others would give us quick glances. The customers looked uneasy as they walked by.

Aganes took a few more steps toward me as he continued, "I should burn this place to the ground. I should kill all of the people here that have been harboring you."

Some of the customers heard Aganes and looked over to him. Not a one looked at him very long without having to look away. His eyes burned with anger and hatred. He was not someone that anyone wanted to make eye contact with.

"They had nothing to do with it," I replied in a lower voice. "Not a soul knows who I am."

"Do not lie to me."

"Please," I said looking into his eyes. "Do not hurt any of them. They did not know."

"Haborym the compassionate," he laughed mockingly. "If only these pathetic souls knew how many died because of you. Why did you change? Why do you care for them? None of them are loyal to you. None of them care about you."

"It is a matter of right and wrong."

"You were supposed to be trained in political science and sociology, not philosophy. We all new philosophy would get in the way. They warped your mind with the thoughts of the free-thinking," he replied. He was only a few feet in front of me.

I looked around to weigh my options. *Should I fight or should I run?* Most of the customers and the cashier had stopped what they were doing and were staring at us. They stared at us like spectators at a prizefight. A battle was about to begin, and they were eager to watch it.

Everything told me to fight, except common sense. I could not defeat Aganes. Seldom few existed who could. I could not run. He blocked the way to the door, and he would catch up to me anyway. I could not persuade him. He was far too set in his ways. I could only surrender. I knew one day I would be caught; it may as well be this day. I could also bargain. Aganes knew how the hierarchy worked, and I knew how Aganes worked.

"I will come with you Aganes…"

"I know that."

"…On one condition."

"You are in no position to…"

"No one else is to be harmed. None of these people know. Not a one."

"Too bad you have nothing to bargain with."

"It would be unfortunate if I had to tell the hierarchy that your pupil knew of my existence before you did. That it was him that caught me, and not you."

"That's not true!" he said, raising his voice slightly. He made his hands into fists and took another step toward me. "That idiot merely stumbled upon you. I am the one who has captured you!"

"It is true enough to begin an investigation. They will bring Sam back, get his story and mine, and see that they are the same. The hierarchy will be incensed. Their wrath will be swift and strong. Punishment for me, and…no promotion for you."

Aganes was furious. I did not have to read it in his eyes, his entire being showed it. He rushed forward and stood directly in front of me. His face was inches from mine. His breath was hot and it had a faint smell of sulfur to it.

"I should destroy you now," he said. "The order stands. Bring him back, dead or alive. They would not mind."

"I think they would," I replied calmly.

Capture was the only way for him to look good. They did not want me dead. They wanted me punished. More importantly, they wanted to do it, not one of their foot soldiers. It was the only thing I had to bargain with.

Aganes stared at me for some time. His anger was not subsiding. He was obviously concluding that I was right. Finally he broke the silence. "Fine. None of these people will be hurt."

"Thank you."

Aganes grabbed my arm and led me out of the marketplace, never giving me a chance to say anything to the employees. It was probably for the better, no reason to give him time to change his mind. His fury showed as he shoved me through the automatic doors. He led me across the parking lot toward the coffeehouse. The sun was almost overhead and its warmth reminded me of my time here. Sam was still in front of the store as we approached.

"Enjoy your time here, Samsapeel," Aganes huffed as we got closer to him.

Sam stared back at Aganes not saying a word. Aganes did not look at him.

Enjoy your time here? Was Sam staying?

Sam turned from Aganes and looked at me. His dark, brown eyes told me everything. I got a read on him immediately. He did not want to return home, he wanted to stay here. In order to do so, he betrayed me. He turned me into Aganes to strike a deal. He looked out for himself. The only one who mattered. No system, no duty, no sacrifice…just reward. He did what any human would do. I lowered my head in defeat.

Aganes led me but a few feet from Sam. Just as I was about to pass, I turned to him, and once again looked him in the eyes. "Of all

the lives that were saved, yours is the one I will remember most."
Sam's eyes blinked as I said my last words. He was probably
wondering what they meant.

Aganes opened the rear door on the car that was in front of the
coffeehouse. He shoved me into the seat. I took one, long, last look
at Sam. Aganes did the same. He said nothing to Sam as he sat down
in the driver's seat of the car and started the engine. He backed out
of the spot and circled around to the road. I could feel Sam watching
us as we drove away. I did not look back. I knew I would never
return here again.

I was coming to terms that my escapade of freedom was over,
when something caught my gaze in front of me. Amy's car pulled into
the parking lot. My heart sank again. The entire week was the best
of my life, and it was all because of her. It was just a few days ago
that she said 'good morning' to me at the coffeehouse. Everything
began to change after that. The movie, the kiss, the poems, all of it
had an effect on me. She had made me into what I wanted to be: a
human being.

I began to cry in the back seat of Aganes' car. Through my tears
I could see a faint smirk on my captor's face. He must have thought
that I was crying for fear of what they would do to me. I could have
cared less about the hierarchy at that moment. Their torture I could
endure, the pain inside me I could not. I was sad that I would never
see Amy again. I was in tears because I would never feel those
emotions again. I was crying because I would never feel the warmth
of her kiss again. I felt cold and empty that I would never get the
chance to say 'thank you' or 'sorry' to her. I was shattered because
I was not sure which one I would have said to her if I had the chance.

Chapter 10
Samsapeel

Amy pulled into the parking lot as Aganes and Magnus drove away. I stood and watched her as she parked next to Jessica. I nodded to Jessica to let her know it was all right to come out. They got out of their cars. Amy appeared to say something to Jessica, but Jessica didn't seem to reply. They walked into the café. I labored to follow them.

"Did you see that car leaving the parking lot? It looked like Magnus was in the back seat with some old man driving," she said very lively. "Maybe his dad came and picked him up for brunch or something?"

"Yeah, maybe," I murmured, as I turned to stare out the window.

"Oh yeah, good morning. You can go home if you want, boss."

Amy hadn't noticed the remnants of my anger. Jessica remained silent. I could feel her staring at the back of my head. Amy continued into the backroom to stash her purse. She came back out front quickly.

"Okay, what's wrong with you two?" Amy asked frankly, as she tied her apron behind her back.

I thought I heard Jessica whimper as the saloon doors to the back room slammed into the doorframe.

"What's wrong?" Amy sounded like she was trying to stop Jessica. She must have gotten a cold shoulder.

I remained staring out the window. The sun loomed overhead. I looked upon it, noticing for the first time how beautiful it can be just to be in its presence. It provided for this world. I saw within its shine, the power to take the place of the fires from my previous life. I heard Amy walking toward me. I checked my reflection in the window to see if my eyes were bloodshot. I noticed they weren't. I turned around just as she was about to grab my arm. I stared blankly at her. I knew I had to tell her. I had to talk with her face to face. I had to tell her what I had done to Magnus. I had to tell her what we were, who we were, where we were from. I had to tell someone. I had to explain to her why she would never see Magnus again. *What would be the consequence of someone knowing the truth about our kind? Would she be in danger if she knew?* I had to tell her these things…

I wasn't sure if I actually could. I thought about Aganes and what he would do to someone if they knew the truth. I thought about what Amy would do if she knew the truth. I thought about what I would do if I told the truth. I was starting to feel that my life at the café was over. I was being forced to move on: by Aganes, by Jessica, by Amy, by Sarah, and by the guilt of what I had done to Magnus.

I gestured toward one of the tables near the front window. I wanted to be close to the sun. It seemed to give me warmth that I'd never been able to feel. I felt that with the sun in front of me, I could do anything. We sat down. She looked very nervous, almost scared.

"Am I fired?" she asked bluntly. She stared me straight in the eyes.

"Huh?" I retorted. Her question took me off guard. "No," I answered. That was the farthest thing from my mind. I wasn't even thinking that I was her manager or boss at that point. I was only thinking of what needed to be revealed to her. *How much did she actually care for Magnus?*

She seemed to relax, but still looked confused. "Then what is going on?"

"How do you feel about Magnus?" I asked, choking as I said his name. I wasn't sure if she would be able to handle what I was going to tell her. I wasn't sure if *I* would be able to handle what I was going to tell her, so I didn't know how to ease into the subject.

"I don't know quite yet. We only had one real date. Two, if you count the open mic night. He is definitely a little weird. Dark and mysterious, though, and I like that. He is very attractive." She seemed to be talking as if she were telling one of her friends about him. She must have realized this too since she abruptly changed her tone. "Wait, why do you care?" she asked inquisitively.

"We have to talk about something that goes beyond our employer-employee relationship and I need to know how you feel about him." I watched her stare blankly at me. I continued before she could say anything else, "I have done something that I was supposed to do many years ago. However, because of my relationships with all of you, I feel that what I have done will leave everyone with an attitude of betrayal toward me." I paused a moment when I saw Jessica walking toward us. It looked like she had been crying in the backroom. I knew she hadn't heard anything that happened between Aganes and me, but she had definitely watched the whole thing, including the abduction of Magnus.

"Jessica, can you please lock the front door, then have a seat with us?" I asked her calmly.

Jessica did as I asked and sat down quietly next to Amy.

I addressed Jessica, "I was just about to tell Amy what just transpired here."

"Okay, boss," said Jessica, sounding like a lump was in her throat.

I continued, "That car you saw leaving the parking lot when you arrived, *did* have Magnus inside. I want to apologize to both of you for what I have done. Magnus was not quite the…person…you may have thought he was. Just as I am not the…person…you may think

I am. We come from a different…" I searched for a proper word, "…culture." I wasn't ready to reveal everything and they didn't need to know.

"What do you mean?" Amy asked. She shook her head in bewilderment.

"That guy looked like he was your father or something," Jessica stated.

Amy said, "Wait," then paused. "Are you and Magnus brothers?"

Her question threw me off guard. Maybe I shouldn't have invited Jessica to sit with us. She had a tendency to believe things according to her own world. She didn't think about things before she talked. Worse still, she was interrupting me during what was probably the hardest thing I had ever had to do.

"No, we're not brothers," I said. I stared straight through Jessica. She looked scared by my eyes and words. She quickly got up from the table. I could hear her muffled sobs as she stormed into the backroom.

"Jessica?" Amy called out. "What in God's name is going on?" she yelled as she turned to look at me. "Who the hell do you think you are? You better tell me what is going on or…or I am…calling the owner. No, I'm going to call the cops."

Part of me understood her questioning. Part of me understood her anger. *What could I say without giving them the whole truth?* I tried to redirect the conversation, "Can I just tell you that I am sorry?" *Can that be good enough? Is that ever good enough?*

"Sorry, for what?" It seemed as if Amy was wondering out loud, looking back and forth from the backroom to me. She had only calmed slightly. She pulled out her cell phone.

"Magnus is never coming back. I don't know if I did the right thing or not, but I know he is gone. For that, I apologize. I apologize, because I know he meant something to you, Amy, even if it was only the beginning stages of a relationship. I apologize, because I know, in his eyes, I have betrayed him. I apologize because I have led you to believe I am someone that I am not…but I am trying to become. Until I can control and overcome the instincts that I learned in my past, I will constantly be a threat to anyone who tries to get close to me," I paused to take a breath. "I realize that now."

Amy sat and stared at me with a confused look on her face. She looked, also, like she was about to cry. I wasn't sure if it was from the confusion or the anger. She looked stunned.

I continued, "You have all taught me so many things about this place. Jessica showed me that order *could* exist here in this world of chaos. That loyalty can occur from respect and not just fear. Amy, you showed me that people *could* find companionship and solace in the strangest and oddest people or places. Sarah showed me how lust and desire can drive humans to do the craziest things. However, now, in the end, I feel you will no longer hold any respect for me. For this, I apologize, as well."

I watched her sit in silence. I wasn't sure if she was the type of person that could even handle the inherent deepness of what I was telling her. My best course of action would probably have been to simply say "goodbye," and leave.

But, I continued, "Magnus told me about all the things that made him want to stay here. He told me why he betrayed my kind in the first place to save all of you. He showed me what the things I was feeling were. He let me know how much you meant to him, Amy. The way he felt for you is represented in me through how I feel about Sarah." I raised my voice, shouting so that maybe Jessica could hear me in the backroom, "Jessica, you showed me how loyal someone can become when they respect someone." I figured she would be listening. I lowered my voice back down, "It is a kind of love, I think."

Amy finally started to cry. Her tears were many and beautiful. That's what I wanted to see. I knew she understood what I was saying. I saw Jessica show her head over the saloon doors, emotionless and silent.

"He let me know how much humanity meant to him. I began to see his point. He began to trust me. We weren't trained to trust people. We were trained to do our jobs, our duty; that was the order we come from. He was arrogant in the end. Maybe he always was, and that is what got him in trouble in the first place." I trailed off. I started to justify my actions out loud. I wasn't doing it for their sake, but for mine. I needed to hear my own thoughts. Jessica came out of the backroom. I motioned for her to rejoin us. She came over and stared at me irreverently before taking her seat.

I reverted back to talking about them, "However, you two have shown me so much. Jessica, maybe in another life we could have been together. We pass through so many lifetimes meeting so many people. We judge so many people throughout our time here. Some we become more intimate with, some we simply pass by. That is what makes us all the same throughout all planes of existence. You have both accepted me into your lives in one-way or another. For that, I am grateful."

"This is all too weird for me to comprehend," Jessica said through her waning sobs.

"This can't be right," Amy wiped the tears from her cheek.

"What are you saying, boss?" Jessica asked curiously.

"I'm saying that I have to go. Over time you may forget that I was ever here. That would probably be for the best. I don't *need* forgiveness, like Magnus did. I simply wanted to apologize to let you know what happened."

"Where are you going?" Jessica asked, tears once again forming in her eyes.

I continued, ignoring her question, "Maybe, in a way, I *am* asking for forgiveness...from Magnus. I don't know."

"I don't want you to go," Jessica pleaded.

"Please tell Sarah I am sorry." I stood up. I pushed my chair in and walked to the front door. I turned my head to take one last look at Amy and Jessica who were both crying at the table. I turned back around and walked out of the café. I had never brought any personal belongings to work so I had nothing to gather. I barely looked at my car as I walked by it in the parking lot.

I walked through the parking lot to the street corner. I stared up at the movie marquee while I waited for the crossing light to illuminate. One day I might actually see a movie, I thought; maybe an animated movie about a fish. It seemed appropriate. The crossing light came on and I walked across the street. A few cars rushed by next to me. The engine noise was overwhelming, yet soothing. I let my head fill with the sounds of the street.

"Boss..." Jessica was right next to me as I made it to the other side of the street. I didn't hear her approach. Somehow I suspected she would follow me, but it was still a little surprising. She grabbed my shoulder from behind and I stopped. "Sam?" I think it was the first time she had ever called me 'Sam."

"Jessica."

"Where are you going?"

Something was beautiful about her eyes—bloodshot and wet from crying.

"Away from this place, Jessica."

Something was beautiful about her lips—red and moist from the tears that collected on them.

"I want to go with you," she said firmly.

Something was beautiful about her cheeks—rosy, but dripping black and blue with mascara.

"I have to go alone. I have to start over somewhere else. I have to fit in somewhere else. Somewhere I am not known."

Something was beautiful about her nose—pink and fighting to hold in its liquid.

"What does that mean?"
Something was beautiful about her voice—sharp, but filled with sobbing lust.
"I don't know. I can't be somewhere where I know I have betrayed those around me."
"Why do you call it betrayal?"
"I turned Magnus in so that I could stay here. I shook his hand, and he trusted me." I raised my voice so that she would understand the necessity of my actions. I needed to push her away.
"Amy will forgive you…" she paused "…I forgive you."
Something was beautiful about her…
I handed Jessica my keys: my car, apartment, and the café. I turned and started walking again, but at a quicker pace. Jessica stood still. I could feel her eyes staring at me as I walked away.
"I won't forgive myself," I whispered as I turned my head to take one last look at Jessica. "I can't…" I waved and kept walking. She didn't follow.
I looked at the sun that was making its afternoon descent. I walked toward it thinking of what I was going to do for the rest of my life here on Earth.

Printed in the United States
47204LVS00002B/9